WILD CHILD

OLIVIA KRIMIN

Midnight Cove Publishing — Indiana, PA
Paperback ISBN: 979-8-8693-5092-3
eBook ISBN: 979-8-3303-0777-7
Title: *Wild Child*
Author: Olivia Krimin
Digital distribution | 2024
Paperback | 2024

Published in the United States by New Book Authors Publishing

DEDICATION

To Grace Louther, who planted the seed, and Jennifer Beer, who nurtured it.

PROLOGUE

A shrill whistle trickled delicately through the forest, the leaves shivering fearfully on their branches, the clouds shifting to engulf the vibrant moon. The clearing was cast in deep, looming shadows that prowled in the night.

Whispers lurked behind trees and amongst the blades of grass, slithered up flower stems and ruthlessly stole the life from their petals. Deceptive and torturous and cruel, those whispers filtered in through the skin of two adults standing in the middle of the clearing. They were swaying on their feet, weighed down by camping gear and other belongings, eyes devoid of life as they stared off into an unknown no other being alive could see. It was as if they were in a trance, anchored by a set of invisible shackles that inhibited backward movement.

The shadows snaked over their forms, aiding the whispers in their influence. Lies, fears, and deranged visions scattered across the adults, the spray of blood at the scene of a crime. They took a simultaneously stilted step forward before jerking to a stop. Something loosened in their consciousness, one memory, then two, then three, until the number amounted to thousands tumbling into the abyss. Tendrils of ancient matter weakly reached out to try to claim them back, to protect them, but were easily thwarted by a carefully constructed lie murmured just so. Free of any more obstacles, the whispers swept the memories away with a careless hand. The shadows, waiting, swallowed them whole, where they ceased to exist at all.

Those shadows reached out into the world with aching hands, reached inside minds that knew nothing of what was to come. The whispers snapped the threads, and the shadows took hold. It was done in an instant, and no one felt a thing.

A single face, a single presence held in common in all of those memories, completely erased. Completely gone. Just like that.

The adults moved forward without any problems after that, as if they were merely taking an evening stroll in the park. Their forms disappeared through the trees, pleasant smiles adorning their lips, something unhinged still residing within the rooms of their eyes.

Abandoned behind them?

A lone navy tent, the front entrance partially unzipped.

Inside that tent?

A little girl of 10 years, hair of fire and eyes of dampened earth, dreaming soundly in a single sleeping bag left behind.

The same whistle came again on a light breeze, the grassy clearing rippling in the silvery light of the reappearance of the waning moon.

The girl curled in on herself, anguish distorting her features, where previously there had been peace, as a small wounded noise left her mouth.

The forest around her rippled with the same movement as the grass, undulating with an odd translucence.

The trap was set, and a low, demented laugh echoing with triumph and hunger resounded from somewhere deep within the trees.

CHAPTER ONE
THE FAMILY TRIP

Kaitlyn became distinctly aware of a gentle mist hitting her face as light slowly lit up the darkness behind her eyelids. She scrubbed at her face, grumbling incoherently before flopping over and burying her head in the blanket.

For a few moments, there was only bliss.

Then something wet, pointy, and *hard* jabbed violently in her ear and she sat up with a yelp, furiously rubbing her offended cartilage against her shoulder.

When the sound of snickering reached her ears, she narrowed her eyes, glancing over to find her big sister waggling a dampened pointer finger at her with a simpering grin.

Snarling, Kaitlyn grabbed her pillow from where, just moments before, she'd been *rudely* awakened from her peaceful slumber, and smacked her sister with it.

"You jerk! Why can't you ever wake me up like a normal person!?" Kaitlyn whined, proceeding to roughly shove her still-grinning sister off the bed.

Blowing a long strand of hair out of her face from her propped position on the floor, Lillian retorted, "Well if you didn't sleep like a friggin' rock, it wouldn't be a problem!"

Kaitlyn harrumphed, crossing her arms and turning her chin up. "You're just jealous because you wake up all the time during the night."

Lilly made a disgusted face. "As if I'd be jealous of a snot-nosed brat!"

She proceeded to grab the pillow from Kaitlyn's hands

and slap her with it.

"Hey!" the younger girl exclaimed indignantly before grabbing a second pillow and launching a merciless barrage on her sister.

The two went back and forth, exchanging hits amidst remarks of mock outrage, laughter, and plenty of "oofs."

"Girls?"

They both froze mid-smack, sharing a wide-eyed look.

"You better hurry," their dad sing-songed, "or else I'll have to feed Teddy all your bacon. He looks pretty hungry."

Shoving Kaitlyn to the floor, Lillian zipped out of the room shouting, "Don't you dare!"

Hauling herself to her feet, Kaitlyn chased after her. "No fair, Lilly! Dad you can't do that! You'll make him fat!" she protested, hurtling noisily down the steps.

She slid into the kitchen, whipping her head around. Sighing with relief upon seeing her bacon unharmed, she dropped into her chair next to Lilly, and dug in.

"Just once, could you not eat like a pig?" Lilly said as she eyed Kaitlyn's messy face with a grimace.

Kaitlyn smiled with her mouth full, and Lilly made a scandalized noise.

"I hope you girls are packed," their mom said as she breezed into the kitchen, ruffling Kaitlyn's hair as she headed toward the rumbling coffee pot.

"Uuuhh," the sisters voiced simultaneously.

Their mom gave the girls an innocent look before glancing at her husband. "That is today, right honey?"

Their dad smirked, casually carrying on with his task of washing the dishes and responding airily, "That's right. The Amor family camping trip. In fact, we're supposed to leave in an hour. It would be a sham—"

Silverware clanked loudly on porcelain plates as chairs scraped against wood, cutting off his sentence. Their dad glanced over his shoulder and found the table empty.

Upon hearing the faint echo of thumping up the stairs, he shook his head and looked over at his wife, who was leaning lazily on the counter with a mug cradled in her hands. She wore an amused expression, and he asked her rhetorically, "What are we going to do with them?"

Pushing off the counter, their mom patted their dad on the cheek. "I'm sure you'll figure it out."

He scoffed, turning back to the sink as she grabbed the plates and glasses off the table and brought them over.

"That's all you y'know. The forgetfulness. They certainly didn't get that from me," their mom teased, nudging her husband gently in the ribs.

"'Least I didn't give them my stubborn disposition," he mused with a challenging glint in his eye.

She raised a groomed eyebrow, pursing her lips, "I hate when you do that.

Their dad's laugh reverberated through the sunlit kitchen, and all was well.

<p style="text-align:center">~~~~~~~~~~</p>

The car was packed before 11 am, and they were all settled in their respective seats when Kaitlyn cried, "Wait!" as their dad started the car.

They all paused as Kaitlyn struggled out of her seat, opened the car door, and ran back to the house. She went inside with the spare key, appearing a few minutes later, re-locking the door and replacing the key.

She ran back to the car and resituated herself, clutching a stuffed dog to her chest.

Lilly raised an unimpressed eyebrow. "Really, you went back for that thing?"

Kaitlyn rolled her eyes. "Yes *really*. And don't act like you don't still sleep with a stuffed rabbit."

Spluttering in her outrage, Lilly exclaimed, "Did you go in my room?! I told you to stay out!"

Kaitlyn blinked. "I don't know what you're talking about."

Lilly whipped her head to her parents as her dad pulled out of the driveway. "Mom!" Lilly whined in appeal."

Their mom craned her head around the headrest of the front passenger seat, lips pursed and eyebrows raised.

"I didn't!" Kaitlyn defended herself.

"Oh? Then you must be very efficient at seeing through walls," her mom mused.

Kaitlyn nodded enthusiastically at the out she was supposedly being given. "Exactly mom! Now you get it!"

Kaitlyn's mom shared a doubtful look with her eldest daughter.

"Kaity, if you're going to lie, at least make it believable," Lilly admonished.

"I'd rather you not lie at all," her mom added with a stern look.

"But I'm not lying! You just said not to go *in* your room, and I never set one foot inside!"

Disbelieving, Lilly guffawed, "Looking inside falls under the category of staying the hell out!"

Crossing her arms and looking out the window with a pout, Kaitlyn mumbled petulantly, "Well, you should be more clear about that next time. Also, that boy over your bed isn't even that pretty, and his music sucks, so I don't know why you listen to him."

Lilly's mouth fell open slightly, offended, before she tentatively looked over at her mom, who was now sporting a second round of raised eyebrows.

"There's more to a person than looks, honey," she informed her youngest daughter diplomatically. "Your dad is a perfect example of that," she added with a sly grin, gesturing with mock elegance toward the male driving the car.

Their dad's responding grin was sharp. "I think I'll pretend I didn't hear that," he said before shooting Kaitlyn a wink in the rearview mirror.

Kaitlyn snorted.

"Mom, what about talent? Is there more to a person than that when they're not good at anything?" Kaitlyn asked, clever eyes flashing.

Her mom blinked, laughing nervously. "Well, I'm sure, I mean... honey, help me out here," Kaitlyn's mom whisper-demanded furtively.

Their dad shook his head and spoke with a taunting lilt, "Oh no you don't, you lost your right to play that card the second you insulted my rugged good looks."

Their mom clicked her tongue and plucked the sunglasses from their dad's face as they paused at a stop light. He made a playful swipe for them, but the light lit up green and an impatient driver honked at them from behind.

Setting the frames over her eyes pointedly, she jerked her chin forward and drawled innocuously, "Don't you have a car to drive?"

He chuckled lowly as he pressed on the gas, shaking his head faintly with a good-natured sigh.

Their mom turned around to look at them again, slipped the sunglasses down her nose, and raised her eyebrows twice in quick succession.

The girls burst into snickers, and their dad smiled as the mom placed the sunglasses carefully back over his eyes.

~~~~~~~~~~

"Are we there yet?" Kaitlyn drawled.

"What does it look like, dingus?" Lilly said shortly, poking at her phone screen with meticulously manicured nails.

Kaitlyn made a spectacle of looking around through all the windows before replying, "It looks like trees, which you camp in. What does it look like to you?"
~~~~~~~~~~

Lilly side-eyed her sister, raising an eyebrow. "It looks like an impatient little nuisance."

Kaitlyn growled, narrowing her eyes in return. She turned away to look out the window, the world a vibrant green blur behind the pane of tinted glass.

"You should try being nicer Lilly, then maybe Damien would stop leaving you 'on read,'" Kaitlyn grumbled, glancing at her sister's reaction in the indistinct reflection of the window.

Before she could stop herself, their mom let out the start of a snort before hastily snapping her mouth shut, eyes wide in horror.

Lilly's face had gone pink, hardly sparing a feigned glance of betrayal at her mom before the teen barked, "You don't know anything you little twat! You're just talking crap."

Lilly reached out and ruthlessly pinched her sister's arm.

Kaitlyn paused to let out a pointed 'ow' before continuing, "I know 'on read' makes you mad, whatever that means, so," she finished flippantly, sticking out her tongue.

There was a pause, then Kaitlyn flicked Lilly on the shoulder.

Kaitlyn raised her eyebrows tauntingly when Lilly turned her head to look at her.

The older teen narrowed her hazel eyes playfully at the apparent challenge. "Hoh? You want war? Fine."

A slapping match proceeded to break out in the back seat, complemented with yelps, laughter, and the occasional squeal.

Their mom, meanwhile, ran an exasperated hand through her lighter hair, casting her blue-green gaze heavenward. "It's been war since I gave birth to them," she mused to no one in particular.

Her husband hummed before he unexpectedly boomed out over the racket, "Hey, don't make me pull this car over!" as he proceeded to turn into the parking lot amidst a grove of trees before pulling into a shaded parking spot.

Both Lilly and Kaitlyn had frozen in the back, Kaitlyn's hand smashed into Lilly's cheek and Lilly's hand tangled mercilessly in the ends of her sister's long hair.

"Gee dad, wahy tuh idle thu-reat." Lilly's remark, slightly inhibited by Kaitlyn's hand, breaking the silence.

Their dad lifted one careless shoulder with that sharp grin of his and promptly exited the car.

Lilly and Kaitlyn shared a skeptical look before snickering to each other.

"Alright, out. Both of you. We've got some camping to do," their mom encouraged, also exiting the vehicle and circling around back.

There was a loaded silence.

"Whoever can carry the most gear to the site the fastest gets the big sleeping bag!" Kaitlyn exclaimed before literally flinging herself out of the car, Lilly shouting her protests as she scrambled in pursuit.

~~~~~~~~~~

They all spent the rest of the day unpacking and setting up camp. Their dad eventually confiscating Lilly's phone, much to Kaitlyn's delight. It had started to become a part of yearly tradition, and Kaitlyn had no qualms about pointing out to her sister that she shouldn't have even bothered bringing it if she knew it was going to be taken away every time.

Their dad would quip merrily that 'old habits die hard' before Lilly ever had a chance to respond. He'd then send Lilly to go collect firewood with their mom and take Kaitlyn with him to stake out their fishing spots along the stream.

The day full of bickering would always soften out the farther the sun descended in the sky. The falling harshness
~~~~~~~~~~

of night broken by tender firelight seemingly having the ability to assuage even the sharpest of tongues, quelling the most insistent of complaints.

They'd all settle around that fire, cocooned in its warm glow. Kaitlyn would make shadow puppets frolic against emblazoned tree trunks, her dad bringing out his own to try and eat hers. Their mom would conjure all her best campfire stories, spin tall tales as high as the embers that danced from the flames. She'd leave them on the edges of their logs, toes curling in their shoes, or roaring with raucous laughter with no in between. Lilly would sing cheesy campfire songs off key just to see Kaitlyn cringe, then start up a genuine tune when she'd had her fun. Their dad would pull out all of his jokes, causing his family to groan in exasperation, though in the end Kaitlyn would snort at one and the other two would give in to their laughter. They'd pass around smores, Kaitlyn catching her marshmallow on fire like her dad, Lilly and their mom lightly roasting theirs with shakes of their heads. Kaitlyn would always end up with chocolate smeared on her face, and Lilly would always call her a pig. Mysteriously, Lilly would find marshmallow stuck in her hair the next morning, and no one really knew how, though Kaitlyn's sticky fingers were always suspect.

When the sky darkened from deep indigo to pitch black, and the stars twirled adoringly around their vast horizon, their parents would always tuck the sisters into their tent before heading to their own. This time was no different.

"Goodnight mom!" Kaitlyn called out once she heard her parents settle in their own tent a little ways away. The embers of the fire still burned dimly, creating a faint orange glow against the nylon of the tent.

"Goodnight Kaitlyn," her mom responded slowly, almost as if she was trying not to smile.

"Goodnight dad!" Kaitlyn continued.

"Goodnight Kaitlyn," he called back in the same tone of voice as her mom.

Kaitlyn paused, turning her head to look at her sister with big eyes.

"*Goodnight Lilly*," she said with purposeful cadence.

The older teen flopped over pointedly. "No."

Kaitlyn huffed, pursing her lips as she rolled over in her *much larger* sleeping bag.

Then their mom called out cheerfully, "Goodnight Lilly!"

Lilly took her pillow and forcefully slammed it over her head, a muffled 'urrrggg' emitting from beneath the fabric a moment later.

The other three family members burst into snickers, and as Kaitlyn got settled in her sleeping bag, she was surrounded by the love of her family. There was a smile on her face when she fell asleep that night, and while no one could see it, Lilly was smiling too.

Though, not long after the last Amor fell asleep, a breeze blew into the clearing, carrying with it an unusually sharp chill. It slithered through tree trunks, over the woodland and the nylon tents before what remained of the fire abruptly extinguished.

Kaitlyn's parent's twitched where they slept.

DAY I:
THE SCRATCHY VOICE

"Mom!? Dad?! ...Lilly!? Where'd you go?!" Kaitlyn wailed, wandering aimlessly around the small clearing where she and her family had established camp the night before. The ground was damp beneath her feet, the grass slick between her toes, likely from rain during the night.

Weak sunlight filtered down through the trees in golden rays, dappling the earth with golden flecks of magic. It was a beautiful place, easily torn right from the pages of a fairytale. But to Kaitlyn, this was far from the make-believe, happy-ending stories she was accustomed to.

Tears gathered in the corners of her eyes, dangerously close to overflowing.

'They have to come back, they just have to. They wouldn't leave me out here...right?'

She gnawed her lip at the thought. She shook her head sharply, mouth thinning into a determined line.

Her tiny fists tightened at her sides, nails digging into soft palms.

'No. Of course they wouldn't. They all love me very much. They probably just went to get something from the car. Yeah, that's it. Except...why would they take everything with them if they planned on coming back?'

She desperately tried not to think about it.

Slowly, she trudged back to the small tent, curling into a fetal position in her army green sleeping bag once she got there. Her tears fell silently, trailing down her throat to soak into the neckline of her nightgown. Not a sound escaped her lips as she waited for her family to come back to her.

<p style="text-align:center">~~~~~~~~~~</p>

Hours passed. The sun sank lower and lower in the sky before dipping below the horizon and then disappearing altogether in a brief, yet brilliant flash of burning gold. Perhaps that was how all things in nature wished for their end to be. Or maybe only the sun was capable of such a dazzling departure.

Kaitlyn's family never returned, and the delicate hope she held to herself began to slip.

"They'll come back. They have to. They wouldn't leave. I refuse to believe it," she spoke aloud to herself, ruthlessly shoving away the plague of doubtful thoughts.

She then busied herself with attempting to relight the remains of the previous night's campfire. She clearly recalled the way her dad had started it, but she soon realized he had had matches.

She didn't have matches.

After the failed attempt to light the charred pile of remains, she shuffled back inside the tent and sat in a tight ball with her knees pulled to her chest and her head tucked down. As she steadily rocked herself, hot tears spilled from her eyes, running searing paths down her face. She couldn't stop the sob that tore itself from her throat. It hurt.

"They'll never come back for you," came a raspy, taunting voice.

'Huh? What was that?'

Kaitlyn peered around frantically in the darkening tent. The voice didn't seem to come from any certain direction, it was sort of just...*there.*

*"It's quite a shame, really. It seemed as though they **truly loved you.**"* The Scratchy Voice heaved a poor resemblance of a sigh, causing a gust of rancid wind to flow through the trees.

It rustled the leaves, the branches creaking chillingly,

throwing ominous shadows along the walls of the tent. An unsettled feeling twisted in her gut.

"Who said that?" Her voice trembled slightly, sounding unnaturally loud in the deafening silence.

She hastily wiped at her damp cheeks and stood up. She crept out of the tent and into the shadowy clearing. The thickness of the trees blocked out the fleeting orange glow hovering on the horizon that the sun left in its wake. She wanted to demand it to come back, as it was the only light she had left and it was abandoning her too, leaving her in the dark just like her family. Never mind that it would return in the morning.

"Not who child, but what~"

"Fine. Then *what* said that?" Kaitlyn demanded in a firmer tone, thankful the waver had fled from her voice.

"That is of little importance to you. You should be **concerned with your family's return, but I suspect they** *are long away from here."*

Something flickered to life within the depths of Kaitlyn's eyes, dancing in the blue-green depths, tender and young, not yet tainted by the cruelty that afflicted the world. It was blind determination and trust that fed that raging inferno.

"You're wrong," she gritted out, words full of conviction, "they wouldn't leave me here. Ever. They'll come back. I'm sure of it." She crossed her arms, chin held high, a daring smile gracing her lips.

'*They'll come back. They have to,*' she reiterated in her head.

"Telling yourself something does not make it true," The Voice seethed.

Seemingly dismissing what The Voice said, she gave a casual shrug. Her expression then morphed into one of inquisition before she asked, "Why is your voice so scratchy? Is there a frog in your throat?"

"No," was all It replied.

She stood in the dark for a few more minutes, listening. When she heard nothing more, she retreated back inside the tent and settled into her sleeping bag.

In the silence of the night and the darkness of the tent, she thought for a long time. About her mom, her dad, and her big sister, Lilly. How her mom always kissed her goodnight, how she would flee to her sister's room after a nightmare and find comfort in those arms, and how her dad always gave her piggy back rides, even if she was getting too heavy for them. Suddenly she was all too aware of the cool, nylon material of the sleeping bag cocooning her, and it was then that she longed for the warm sheets of her bed. She eagerly anticipated her return home, even if it had only been two days since she'd last been there.

With that thought she drifted off into a fitful slumber.

She never heard the soft, cryptic words of The Voice that were whispered in her ears. How its tone took on a strange, almost hypnotizing lilt, how those words held dangerous potential, thoroughly entangling themselves inside her head, making a home in the dark crevices of her mind and settling in for the long winter.

*"You will always be alone, Kaitlyn. You cannot run. **You cannot hide from me. Nothing will save you from the** iron grasp of solitude. Not even the wolves."*

<h1 style="text-align:center">CHAPTER TWO</h1>
BAD DREAM?

Kaitlyn awoke to the sound of indistinct yelling and the eeriness of twilight.

Initially, she was unable to decipher what the person was yelling, but as she quickly exited the tent and scurried to the tree line, the words became deafeningly clear. They sounded as if they were being whispered in her ear, yet still being shouted from a great distance.

"Kaity!? Kaity, where are you?!"

Her heart nearly froze in her chest, before picking back up in quick, sporadic thumps.

'Is that who I think it is?' she thought as her heart swelled with joyful hope in her chest.

"Lilly?! Is that you?! It's Kaity, I'm right where you left me!" Kaitlyn shouted, hearing her voice carry into the forest. It sounded otherworldly as it echoed through the churning air.

Lilly's response came immediately. "Kaity? I can hear you, follow my voice!"

Without hesitation, Kaitlyn charged into the forest. The oddness of the fog was lost on her, smothering the ground thick and heavy, blocking out the black sky above. How the air seemed to glimmer with an unusual luminescence and take on a purple haze.

The trees were spaced closely together with hardly enough room for even a relatively slim person to squeeze through. Despite this, ten-year-old Kaitlyn faced minimal trouble slipping between the rough trunks. She nearly face-planted on more than one occasion, the fog limiting her vision and dulling her senses. The fog was so dense she strained to see her hands in front of her face. But her body was lithe and agile, in the early stages of youth with quick reflexes and nimble feet. A little fog was not going to stop her.

"Lilly, I'm coming! Keep talking!"

"Kaity I'm here, I'm so sorry I left you!"

Kaitlyn continued to race through the woods toward her sister's voice. Stray branches continuously clawed at her face, fog clinging possessively to her skin as if trying to deliberately slow her down, to swallow her whole. She ignored it all with a triumphant smile, feeling as if she was dancing on air with the idea that her sister had come back for her.

'Hah! In your face, stupid Scratchy Voice! I knew they would come back to me.'

Her nightgown snagged on a branch jutting out from a bush. She impulsively yanked as hard as her small body would allow and managed to free herself with a resounding *rip*.

The momentum had her arms pinwheeling as she stumbled back a few steps before completely, ungainly, keeling over backwards. She hit the ground with a quiet 'oof' escaping her lips.

She lay splayed on her back for a moment, trying to catch back the breath that was forced from her lungs. With a huff of annoyance, she quickly hopped to her feet and was running again, her breath now coming in harsh pants.

It wasn't long before she saw a faint figure through the fog and the thinning trees.

"Lilly!" Kaitlyn ran toward her sister, outstretching her arms as she drew near.

Lilly's face lit up. "Kaity!"

Kaitlyn threw herself into her sister's arms, expecting warm, solid flesh. However, her eyes widened in surprise as she was greeted with empty air, body continuing to fall forward.

She tripped over her own feet, held in the grasp of shock, and just managed to keep herself upright as she stumbled through the space where Lilly should have been.

She whipped around, her brow furrowed, and felt her mouth fall slack as she watched her sister evaporate into a fine mist and blend with the swirling fog.

'No...!'

'No...no, it can't be...she was *right there...she–she was* right there!'

Kaitlyn's world started to spin, her heart beating too fast, her breaths coming too hard. The fog was suffocating, clouding all she knew into obscurity. She searched around herself frantically, but there was no sign of her sister. Only white. Cold, stifling, blinding white in her ears, in her mouth, in her nose. She couldn't breathe. It hurt her throat. It all melted together. The ground fell away and then her hands were buried in her hair, yanking, as if she could pull herself from this living nightmare. There was noise roaring in her ears. Ringing. Static. Whispers. They were everywhere, screaming at her until she herself was screaming with them. Her hands slipped from her hair to her ears, viciously shaking her head, as it grew unbearably louder...louder, *louder.* Then it stopped, leaving nothing but a dull ringing within her ears.

She was wheezing and couldn't fathom why. Her head was pounding and she didn't know why...why? ...*why*?!

'*Wha-what's going on...Where am I? I feel dizzy...is the world supposed to be swimming? Or is that the fog?*'

She saw things in that fog, writhing and moving just beyond where she could focus. Black, wicked things that wanted her blood.

'*...or are those trees? They look like trees...maybe this is what Aunt Sarah felt like when they took her away kicking and screaming...*'

She was drowning, being devoured from the inside-out, and trying as she might to suppress it, the tightness in her chest and her frantic thoughts only intensified with the passing seconds.

"L-Lilly?" she choked through her stuttering breath and clouded mind.

No answer.

She grimaced as her head throbbed painfully, crying out with the severity of it. She felt like she was grasping onto the ledge of a cliff and her fingers were slipping. The fog was too bright, it–it was too bright! Her vision swam and her mind was filled with jumbled nonsense and incoherent thought. It was all around her. In her. Consuming her.

'I have to get out, I have to find Lilly! I can't stay here!'

"Lilly, where are you? Please come back! Don't leave me here! Please don't leave me alone! *Lilly!*"

Her voice broke, coming out coarse and uneven as she continued to wheeze. The ground began to tilt more violently than before, and she couldn't keep her knees from buckling. She collapsed to the ground as a wretched sob ripped itself from her chest.

As if It had been waiting in the mist all along, The Scratchy Voice spoke, ***"They never loved you, Kaitlyn. Not mommy, not daddy and certainly not your sister. You will never be loved. You will** always be alone."*

Kaitlyn's hands were slammed back over her ears for the second time that night. "No! Stop it! It's not true! You're lying!"

*"Believe what you wish. Think what you will. But you **feel it. Deep down in that weak, naive little soul, you** feel it. You know I speak the truth."*

She violently shook her head, her whole form thrashing from side to side as if she were having a seizure. "No, get out! Get out of my head! Leave me alone!"

"No...I like it here," It came smugly.

Something in Kaitlyn snapped, bursting to the surface through the fog and whatever evil that had taken hold. The scream that burst forth from her was comparable to the wail of someone who had lost everything, filled with anguish and rage that burned a hot, bloody trail through her veins.

"I said **get out**!"

Everything went black.

DAY 2:
SURVIVAL SPOT

Kaitlyn jerked upright inside the tent; her breathing labored. It came in short, jagged puffs, her body drenched entirely in sweat.

The contents of her dream–or more accurately a nightmare–gradually drifted to the forefront of her mind as she came into full consciousness. Tears, unbidden, burned along her bottom lashes, slowly trickling over as she recovered all the fine details. Soon the tears were falling faster, morphing into sobs and pathetic hiccups. It was the ugly kind of crying–that's what Lilly called it–with the snot and tears running together to create some gross, hybrid funk that everyone experiences, yet few actually admit to.

Despite the cloudiness of her mind, she could only begin to wonder what it all meant.

'It seemed so real. I swear Lilly was really there...'

When her breathing became less erratic, when the heaving of her shoulders ceased and her tears turned to sniffles with only the occasional hiccup, she dared to venture out into the grassy clearing. The sun weaved its warm rays through the branches to bathe the open space in a shining, speckled yellow haze.

The grass was soft beneath her bare feet, the breeze gentle on her exposed skin. She wore a simple cotton, lavender colored nightgown with pretty lace frills around the tanked sleeves. She wiggled her small toes through the twitching blades of green.

She realized for the first time how beautiful the clearing was, the way the light filtered through the leafy branches of the Oregon White Oaks and Sitka Spruce trees. The way the air smelled faintly of pine and sap, the way the wind rustled through the trunks and stirred up leaf litter on the ground. Perhaps it was telling a secret...perhaps it was telling a lie.

There was a single cluster of flowers a few yards away from her, where the grass gradually faded to dirt at the edge of the clearing. From it sprouted three thin stems with tiny leaves. At the tip of each, a dainty baby blue flower bloomed. It almost looked lonely.

She smiled for the first time since she woke up alone. It was small, but it was there.

'Baby Blue Eyes,' she thought fondly, *'though it's weird to see one this late in the year.'*

She'd originally been too preoccupied to take in the slightest aspect of her surroundings, but now it was near impossible to overlook. It was strange how she could feel so at peace in that moment, given her current situation. She found her stare drifting off into the trees, her eyes vacant as she gazed into the silent forest.

She might have been looking for something that only she would ever be able to see.

Whatever it was, she never found it.

Her attention was drawn elsewhere as the wind ruffled her hair, her very *tangled* hair. A rat's nest, as her mom would say.

It was a deep red auburn, wavy, and thick, taking on an amber sheen when the sun decided to hit it just right. It reached just past her hips, normally falling in graceful waves down her back, but was presently frizzy and full of an endless array of knots.

She attempted to comb her fingers through it but found the action futile.

Her stare drifted absentmindedly toward the ground, and that was when she froze.

There was a tear in her nightgown.

Her heart started to pound.

Her thoughts began to race.

'Wait...what...? How...? Does that mean...it wasn't...a dream?'

Her breath started to pick up. She tried to calm it.

'No ...No. No. No. How is that even possible? How could I have woken up in my tent if I was out in the woods? It doesn't make any sense!'

It was then that Kaitlyn's stomach decided it would like to impress mother nature with its imitation of a humpback whale. If there had been someone else around to hear, she might have been inclined to feel some sort of embarrassment.

"Still believe your family is coming back for you?"

Kaitlyn managed to suppress her instinctive urge to startle, instead placing a hand firmly on her hip and shifting her weight to the side, an unimpressed look taking over her elfin features that displayed a level of precociousness befitting of her older sister's age rather than her own.

"As a matter of fact, I do. I have complete faith that mom and dad will come back for me."

Though, even as she spoke, something cold trailed its spindly fingers up her spine.

'That dream...what if they never come back? What will I do then?'

The darkness was there, hovering, waiting, but it didn't get the chance to sink its teeth in, not yet.

'No. I have to stay positive. It's what mom always says. What I had was just a dream. That's it. Nothing more. I probably just ripped my nightgown yesterday and didn't notice until now.'

"How many times must reality be spoken for it to blunder through your thick, childish head? They don't love you! They abandoned you!"

Her response was immediate and filled with a heated certainty, "They *do* love me. What I just had was a bad dream. That's all. They'll come back. And my head's not thick, you...you big butt face! You're just like Chelsea, the bully from my school."

Kaitlyn stared off into the woods again once she finished talking. It was August 14th when she and her family had arrived at the campsite. A Sunday. It had been two days since then, making today a Tuesday.

"Hope is a dangerous thing, child, and your pathetic existence reeks of it."

Its voice was chilling, words dark and daunting, but Kaitlyn kept her expression blank, attempting to appear unfazed. She continued on as if all was right with the world.

"Scratchy Voice, you're silly! Hope can't be dangerous, it's not a solid thing," she informed as she began walking at a casual pace toward the tree line.

"Then answer me this, Kaity dear: if hope is not a **corporeal thing, then why do you humans cling to it as** *if it is the only thing that will save you?"*

Kaitlyn's voice turned harsh, unyielding even, as she stopped abruptly in front of the line of trees. "Don't call me Kaity. Only my sister can call me that. And what do you even want from me? You keep saying that my family doesn't love me and that they're not coming back, but what do you know!? You're just a stupid Voice that came out of nowhere trying to confuse me! Just stop it already. It's not. Going. To work. So go away."

After a second, she added curtly, "Please."

Kaitlyn harrumphed to herself immediately after.

'Stupid Kaitlyn,' she chastised herself, *'being polite to things that don't deserve it.'*

She listened out into the woods. Much to her surprise, she thought she heard the sound of running water.

'How did I not notice until now?' she thought to herself.

Continuing in ominous cadence as if she hadn't spoken, The Voice seethed, *"Because if they do **not, they have** *nothing. When humanity has nothing, it turns on itself, just as you will when you realize you have no reason to keep going."*

Kaitlyn didn't respond, doing her best to prevent the words from affecting her and shutting them out. But in they crept, slowly seeping into her mind. They collided with something there, something tender. Then they slithered their way down her throat and settled firmly in the pit of her stomach. She felt her windpipe compress and a pound of rocks drop unmercifully into her gut. Deep down she knew better, and strived to bury it so far inside her that she would forget its existence.

She stepped past the tree line and began walking at a leisurely pace. The trees weren't as densely packed here, so she could travel through them with ease, the only sound being the light crunching and snaps of her feet on the branches littering the ground. Sometimes the broken twigs pricked the sensitive skin there, but she continued her trek anyway.

She'd been walking for several minutes when she stopped dead in her tracks, wondering how it'd taken her so long to realize.

Everything looked the same.

'Why did it all look the same?'

Her head started to spin.

Her feet picked up the pace without her telling them to. It wasn't long before she was sprinting, her line of thought turning frantic.

'What's going on?! Why is nothing changing? It looks the same way it did when I first passed the tree line!'

"No chosen child ever leaves this forest," came the low hiss of The Voice.

Kaitlyn's eyes widened, feeling a twinge of unease pierce through her chest, her heart beating hard and fast. *'Chosen!? What does It mean by 'chosen'?'*

Breathless and thoroughly rattled by this new

information, she stumbled to a halt. The sound of rushing water was much louder now, almost as if it were right in front of her. She'd worry about the 'chosen' thing later.

"It's not real, whatever's happening. I can hear the water. It's right beside me and you're just trying to throw me off." She closed her eyes, almost immediately reminded of the way Dorothy clicked her heels in the Wizard of Oz, how she said 'There's no place like home' three times and was miraculously returned there.

Kaitlyn figured that there was no harm in trying, only instead of going home, she'd make the water appear.

She took a deep, steadying breath. "It's not real." She tapped her heels together.

"It's not real." She tapped them again.

She squeezed her eyes shut tighter, her hands clutching into the fabric of her nightgown so hard it was a wonder it didn't tear. "It's *not* real." She tapped her heels a final time.

Kaitlyn felt a rush of air billow her hair back like a cape, her eyes fluttering open in response. What she saw drew a silent gasp from her lips. Before her had appeared a flowing stream, bubbling and blue as it glided over moss covered stones.

She was surrounded by the same piece of forest as before, only in this spot there was water traveling for as far as the eye could see as it winded around the base of the tree trunks, some of the twisted roots growing into the cool brook. Unlike the rest of the forest, there were several bushes scattered along the bank on both sides of the stream. They appeared to be berry bushes, berries that were small, bumpy, round, and reddish pink in color.

She allowed herself a sigh of temporary relief as she rushed forward and collapsed to her knees on the spongey, slightly rocky ground of the riverbank. She stretched her arms out until they were hovering over the lazily drifting rapids near the center of the stream before dunking her hands under the small white crests of the cold water, quickly bringing her cupped hands to her mouth. She slurped noisily, could hear her mom's voice in her head calling her unladylike, but she had failed to realize how thirsty she was until the liquid was sliding down her throat.

When watching survival shows with her dad, she remembered seeing the people take water from the middle of a moving body of water; it was the cleanest there because it was constantly moving.

After drinking her fill, she wandered over to one of the bushes, eyeing it curiously as she noticed the pinkish berries. She supposed they were raspberries.

'*Yuck.*' she thought, outwardly cringing at the thought of eating one.

But her mom always said 'beggars can't be choosers,' so she sucked it up and reluctantly reached for one.

As her hand drew near, she abruptly felt a sharp sting.

"Ow!" she yelped shrilly, hastily bringing her finger to her lips. Her mouth tasting like she'd just licked a metal pole, she withdrew her finger to assess the damage. There was the daintiest of gashes on the tip of her index finger. Scarlet welled up and formed a small bead on her skin, threatening to pop. She sucked on her finger again and glared at the bush as if it had personally offended her, which, technically, it had.

As she looked closer, she saw that the stems and branches were covered in fine, hair-thin thorns and that the leaves of the berries were rather pointy. Rolling her eyes at her own recklessness, she exercised more caution as she plucked a berry off the bush and held it between her forefinger and thumb, regarding it blandly.

She gave it a precarious sniff, a frown on her face.

Huffing in defeat Kaitlyn squeezed her eyes shut and popped the berry in her mouth before she could talk herself out of it. She scrunched her nose as she chewed, almost gagging at the slimy texture in her mouth combined with the crunchy seeds.

It took more effort than what should've been necessary, but she eventually made herself swallow. She shook herself once the action was done, shivering at the thought of repeating the process.

She forced them down anyway, her stomach beginning to churn.

She debated on carrying some back to the tent, but decided against it as she could just come back the next day.

She turned away from the berry bush, taking a moment to wipe her mouth, and proceeded to walk back the way she came. When she crossed the tree line, she felt the brief sensation of walking through something cool and fluid.

Perplexed, she whipped around, only to see that the stream was no longer there.

She tilted her head to the side, her brows furrowing. *'What the...where'd it go?'*

A slight movement in front of her caught her eye. A ripple of air, a glimmer that wasn't supposed to be there.

She moved her face closer, realizing the air seemed to pulsate as it undulated before her.

She peered at it with interest, eyes alight with asinine curiosity. Given her current situation, she couldn't afford to be careless, and this thing in front of her screamed all kinds of weird. She should've just walked back to the campsite and ignored it until tomorrow.

So naturally, she warily lifted her foot and thrust it into the churning wall in front of her.

Said foot disappeared in an instant up to her ankle. She automatically yanked her foot back, completely jarring herself and causing her to stumble backward.

She snapped her head down to look at her bare foot, sighing gently when it appeared unharmed. She flexed, pointed, and rotated it a few times for good measure.

'Seems okay...' she thought skeptically.

She had a hunch on what was going on after the vanishing act her foot had pulled, and before she could talk herself out of it, she hurled herself forward and through the-whatever the invisible thing was.

Though she expected it, she still gasped as the stream materialized in front of her.

"Oh look-*y, the wretched child found a survival spot. How fun,*" The Scratchy Voice mocked in Its unsettling lilt.

"What's a survival spot?" Kaitlyn shouted into the woods.

She didn't get an answer.

Kaitlyn sucked her teeth in annoyance, making a 'tch' sound before stomping back through the water-like veil that concealed the so-called 'survival spot.' She was shocked all over again upon seeing the stream disappear as she passed though the veil.

She continued to pace back and forth between the forest and the stream to ensure her vision wasn't playing tricks, her mind reeling all the while.

'How is this even possible? It's like some kind of barrier that separates the 'survival spot' or whatever from the loop forest. Apparently, I 'found it.' What does that even mean? This is crazy. All of it. I'm not supposed to be here! I'm supposed to be at home with everyone watching TV, making Lilly play board games with me, reading books or playing catch with dad out back, not out here in these stupid woods with no one! Why did they leave me out here!? They're supposed to love me! What did I do wrong?'

'Or...what if I...didn't do anything wrong?'

Somehow that was worse.

She started running. She didn't know where or why–she didn't know anything. She just needed to get away. The fear was chasing her, the doubt, the questions she couldn't answer, and it was gaining, gaining, gaining. She was running from the very thing she would never be able to escape from. Because it was all there, it was all inside *her*. Always one infuriating step ahead, no matter what she did. It would always be there, in the back of her mind, in the pit of her stomach, in the rooms behind her eyes when she met her reflection. It had power over her, and she couldn't do a thing about it.

Over the roaring of her ears, she heard the scratchy buzz of The Voice sneering Its sinister words.

*"Your own thoughts will rip you to shreds. I **will enjoy watching you slowly succumb to the monsters inside** your head."*

Then It started laughing. Loud, maniacal laughing, and laughing, and more laughing. It drowned out her screaming mind, bursting in with vicious abandon. Her efforts to fight back were pointless. Because It got in. It got in every single time. Whether she was always aware or not, It was there, nesting, festering, *growing*.

Terror pierced her veins with the unforgiving nature of a bitter winter. She was scared beyond comprehension, lost in an endless maze of thorny hedges and greasy shadows. It rattled her entire being. Goosebumps raced over her skin, her palms starting to sweat, dread forcibly gripping the base of her neck. For the first time in her life, she truly thought she was going to die.

Somehow in her frenzy she managed to make it back to the tent.

She frantically ripped open the flap and threw herself in, burrowing into her sleeping bag and yanking the material over her head, fretfully curling into herself and burrowing her head into the fabric.

She exploded in tears and sobs as her entire body shook violently, desperately attempting to eradicate the ghastly thoughts from her head.

She remained in that position until the world was cast in deep shadows and then into complete and total blackness. She compacted herself even further, knees pressing into her throat. When the whispers began, she didn't fight. Just let The Voice and Its poisonous lies lull her to sleep.

"Don't worry child, you will *soon accept your fate. You can only fight for so long before you tire, and when you fall, I will be there to catch you. Into The Darkness you will go, just like all of those before, just like all of those yet* to come."

Maybe The Voice had a small victory that night.

Maybe Kaitlyn never stood a chance. Or maybe she'd win. Only time would tell.

CHAPTER THREE
WILD

Months came and went. Sometimes quickly, sometimes—most times—more slowly. Kaitlyn followed the passing days with pieces of sticks. Each time the sun sank below the horizon, she added another twig to her pile.

She eventually fell into a monotonous routine, day after day, week after grueling week.

She would wake up from a night filled with terrors, travel to the hidden river, drink and eat her fill of water and the awful berries, and then retreat to her campsite.

She continued to believe her family would return for her, or that she would find a way to escape. When her dreams weren't filled with evil, ungodly things, her parents and her sister were there. Always just out of her reach, nothing but a figment of her pitiful imagination.

They would talk to her too. At least, she thought they did. Their mouths moved, but all she heard was static silence. She could never fully reach them. When she grew too close, they would fall away, shatter into the void with smothered screams pleading for her to help them.

Now those dreams were far and few between, each one that did come, a little dimmer, a little duller than the one before. She blatantly refused to consider what it might mean. Seeing her family, reality or not, had motivated her and reinforced her strength, the doubts sliding reluctantly to the recesses of her mind. As she started encountering them less frequently while she slept, she had to use her own means to continue pushing forward, the burden of survival falling more heavily upon her sagging shoulders. Perhaps the image of her family and her home was enough in the beginning, but it could only drive her so far.

She had to want it. She had to want to survive, to see her family in the flesh again.

But the longer she remained in the wilderness, the more energy she had to expend, the more lies she had to weave on convincing herself why she even bothered to get herself by.

And it was hard. It was hard to rely so heavily on faith when they still hadn't come back...

...when she was still alone.

Well, not *entirely* alone.

The Voice seldomly left her be for very long. It tormented her day in and day out, wore her down to nothing but flimsy threads. And yet, it was still one foot in front of the other.

It began to let things slip, pieces of information that made her wonder what really happened the night before she found herself in her aloneness, why her parents left at all and what drove them away, if The Voice had had a role in it somehow.

Her thoughts often turned to the kids before her. How many? How many times has her situation happened to other kids? What happened to them and where were they? Did they make it back to their families? Did their families come back for them? Or did they...?

No sooner had the thoughts taken shape were they thoughtlessly shoved away. Her questions only brought more burning questions, ones she didn't have the answers to, nor desired to ponder any potential ones either.

The subject matter of the other kids led her to consider The Voice's use of the word 'chosen' on her second day in the forest. She had yet to receive a clear answer, much to her frustration, but it wasn't realistic to expect anything different either. This was The Voice after all. The conclusion she eventually came to was that there wasn't anything particularly exceptional about being 'chosen.' Her best guess was that it meant that if you were a child under a certain age and came into the forest alone or with a family, you were automatically 'chosen' by The Voice. Whether that interpretation was accurate or not would likely remain forever unknown. All she knew was that being selected probably didn't have any sort of deep meaning with roots trailing back to birth, which was what originally troubled her. If The Voice's vague, practically insignificant statements were anything to go on, that didn't appear to be the case. The notion slipped from her mind easily enough, and she decided not to waste any more of her energy on thoughts that weren't productive. In the end, she would only drive herself into madness if she kept it up.

So, she carried on, focusing on her utmost priorities of taking it one day at a time, getting out of the desolate forest, and blocking out The Voice to the best of her ability.

The days steadily grew colder, some of the trees gradually turning from green to yellow to orange to red to brown before falling off completely. With the cold came the infrequent snowfall, a lot of rain and somber clouds. She eventually came to dread the nights as it became a rare sight to see the sun.

The stream never froze, strangely enough, not even near the bank. The berries...well the berries rotted away before the end of September. Which left her to scrounge for other sources of food.

On Kaitlyn's seventh birthday she'd received a book about the edible wild plants of Oregon as a present. It had been the only thing she'd asked for that year.

She read that book from cover to cover exactly three times, and it wasn't exceptionally difficult to recall the knowledge she'd obtained. She was limited though, with the loop forest and all. On a good day she would find a few stalks of beargrass or a clump of bittercress. Oftentimes she returned to her tent with a painfully empty stomach.

She gave hunting a try, too. The presence of animals was near nonexistent, also courtesy of the loop forest, no doubt. She did manage to spot a few critters, mostly squirrels or chipmunks. Not a bug in sight though. That left her scratching her head for a while.

She would score the repeated forest floor, searching for a sharp stick. It didn't take her very long to recognize the same problem: they were the same sticks appearing on loop.

She began breaking branches off the oaks, snapping them until they were sharp enough to use as spears.

Her self-evaluation stated she was a mediocre hunter at best, and that was putting it nicely.

The Voice called her awful, plain and simple.

She was always too loud when she walked, even when she genuinely attempted to be quiet, often scaring the furry creature off before she was even within striking distance. One would've thought that with squirrels came acorns.

They thought wrong. She never saw one.

She scratched her head at that, too.

One day, after one too many failed attempts, she threw her stick down and stomped noisily back to her tent where she proceeded to virgin curse out the stupid forest and the stupid lack of animals and the stupid Voice and her stupid loudness.

It wasn't long before The Voice began to taunt her, to whisper degrading things in her ears. It was enough to send her right back out of that tent to try again.

There was never a repeat of that scenario. She didn't dare openly give up like that a second time, she couldn't afford to.

She spent the next few days moping over her slip up

before knocking some sense into herself and brainstorming a new gameplan.

She first contemplated fishing, but there was not a breath of life in that stream.

So, instead of finding a better way, maybe *she* just had to be better.

Over the course of a week in early October, she practiced silencing her tread, remembering how the participants would walk in the survival shows.

Before the month was out, she caught a squirrel.

Though she neglected what came after the catch:

Cooking it.

She once again recalled what she'd seen on TV. Some individuals had opted to start a fire by striking two stones together—flint, or at least rocks that contain it.

She eventually found herself back on the bank of the stream, eyes scrutinizing the shallow water, and hammocking as many of the wet stones as she could in her nightgown, leaving a large damp spot on the fabric.

She left them to dry in the sun, even doing a little fanning dance around them in the hopes to dry them faster. Though she was certain the only thing she accomplished was looking like a weirdo.

It was by the stroke of a miracle that her haul contained two stones that were sufficient.

By nightfall on the same day she made her catch, she had a fire burning. Pitiful, but it was something.

Over the next few months, with the new addition of fire, Kaitlyn became relatively efficient at thwarting The Voice during the daytime.

It was the night that posed another obstacle entirely.

When darkness fell, the shadows roamed, and the temperatures plummeted. It wasn't uncommon for her to wake up to sooty, black claw marks slashing down the outside of the tent. Sometimes, she'd rouse to discover massive contusions littering her body or jagged, angry scratches across her stomach or back. She often wondered if each night she laid her head down would be the last time she closed her eyes.

Lilly had frequently tried to scare Kaitlyn with the idea of shadow people, how they'd stand at the end of her bed and watch her sleep or drag her off into nothingness if she let her foot hang out from the covers. It was those times where Kaitlyn had found herself with many sleepless nights, but she had a feeling that whatever was clawing at her tent was much, much worse than those shadow creatures her sister taunted her with.

In the dark she felt lost, no light to guide her home.

In the dark she was smaller, weaker. She couldn't withstand The Voice or the shadow demons, couldn't fend off Its whispers and phantom hands that tried to hurt, and she couldn't stop It from invading her soul like a bloodsucking parasite.

It seeped through the cracks of her fragile mind. In the dark, It thrived.

In the dark It fed.

It brought her fears to life, amplified her doubt, emboldened her dread.

In the unfathomable void of night, she didn't fight that Voice.

Merely endured the seemingly endless waves of whispers that led to her fear, led to her doubt, that nearly drove her mad.

She refused to cry during those times, soldiering through every night, each one more nightmarish than the last.

She found solace in thoughts of her family when she wasn't sleeping.

Sometimes it helped.

Sometimes it made things worse.

By the time the snow started to fall in between large bouts of rain in December, she was no longer just a girl, but some hybrid of man and beast, a lurking undertone of feral rage.

She came to understand that in the wild being the polite, well-behaved and civilized daughter she was raised to be, would only inhibit her. The wild didn't play nice. It didn't afford anyone the chance to recover after a blow. You must learn to fight back despite the unfairness.

There were no rules out here. If she did not do what had to be done, then she was as good as dead.

That sweet, naive little girl from a sheltered, urban life wasn't going to save her or get her out of those woods.

Being alone out in a forest trapped in an incessant loop, abandoned by the people who were supposed to care about you, and constantly being harassed by an unknown voice that materialized out of thin air claiming you were going to die did things to a person...

Kaitlyn's family wasn't overtly religious, but she once recalled a time where she was a fervent believer of the man in the sky who created life as everyone knew it.

She wasn't sure what she believed anymore.

Couldn't comprehend what deity out there would let this happen to her.

What she'd done to deserve...this.

She considered that it was her fault but discarded the notion as soon as it had come. She didn't need The Voice latching onto *that* particular thought, seeing as It was already giving her more grief than normal recently.

Although, there was one thing she could--but never verbally would--thank The Voice for.

It kept her alert. Her interactions with It stimulated her mind and heightened her senses, keeping her family at the forefront so she didn't regress into total savagery.

She doubted that was The Voice's intention, but she would count all the blessings that she could.

Besides, a little fear was a good thing. It encouraged caution.

Nothing could possibly sneak up on her.

Nothing.

It was insignificant how much she resented, how much she *hated* that Voice with Its hurtful taunts, infuriating mind games, and sinister promises when It was probably the only thing that anchored her to her waning humanity.

Perhaps It played a role in her survival in the beginning, making her want to prove It wrong.

Whatever the case, it didn't matter, just as long as she stayed motivated.

She decided not to think about it anymore.

So, she turned her attention to the trees.

Turns out they never seemed to end either.

She had invested an entire day climbing tree after tree with her efforts failing to amount to anything substantial. They behaved in a similar manner to the rest of forest. If she climbed ten feet up, it appeared as if another ten feet had been added to the top of the tree. She would rise further from the ground, but when she gazed up it seemed as if she hadn't climbed any height at all.

When the worst of the cold rolled in on frigid gusts of wind, she couldn't afford to divvy space for anything other than survival. Oregon winters weren't typically extraordinarily cold, but in only a thin nightgown, she might as well have been wearing her birthday suit in the middle of a Minnesota January.

Over the months her body had become frail, nothing but skin and bones. With the bitterness of the fastly approaching winter, she became fatigued, her joints noticeably stiffening.

Fire could only do so much.

She constantly kept herself moving, whether it was bouncing on the balls of her feet or jogging circles around the frosty clearing.

The circles beneath her eyes grew darker with each new

day. She could no longer prevent The Voice from invading her head. It simply took too much of the effort she couldn't afford to spare. The jagged scratches curving across her skin came more frequently, no memory of when they first emerged. The shadow demons must have been more subtle than she thought. She couldn't imagine her body could take much more of their abuse, but she'd yet to figure out what she could do about it. The thought of the shadows sneaking up on her like that often left her hyperventilating in the confines of her sleeping bag, so she discontinued any thinking regarding the matter.

As winter's intensity began to accumulate near the end of December, her body fell into an impending state of numbness. Her nightgown, riddled with holes and tears collected over the months provided her with no warmth. She wholly relied on the fire and sleeping bag when she found herself at a rare standstill.

When her fingers began to adapt a blueish-purple tinge, the alarm she knew she should have felt abandoned her. She was able to deduce that it was a bad sign but couldn't be bothered to conjure up a reason as to why. Meanwhile, The Voice skulked in the shadows, waiting.

...It happened on the night of the 26th of December. Kaitlyn should've been with her family snuggled up by a warm fire. Instead, she was fighting for the life that was being tauntingly siphoned out of her.

It wasn't supposed to happen.

She hadn't meant to fall asleep.

Everything had begun to tingle; She felt warm.

She hadn't felt warm for a long time.

She was comfortably curled into a ball in her sleeping bag, the fire long since burnt to ash.

She couldn't help that the soft, twisted nothings The Voice murmured in her ears reminded her so much of the lullaby her mom would sing to her when she had trouble falling asleep. How soft those inky shadows felt as they cocooned around her.

> *~The night is quiet, these stars come and go.*
> *As the moon shines down upon you,*
> *With their ancient silver glow.*

> *Lay down your head and close those heavy eyes.*
> *Let your dreams pull you close.*
> *Your mind can float away.*

> *Release all your fears, for all is right here.*
> *The night won't let you go astray.*

> *I'll protect you dear,*
> *Nothing will hurt you here~.*

She drifted off to the sound of her mom's voice in her ear with a small smile on her face, wheezing shallow puffs of mist from cracked, blue tinged lips.

She never heard the triumphant, manic laughter coming from all directions, never felt it start to drown her in its shadows or the feeling of phantom teeth sinking into flesh.

The following morning would present a revival.

From within The Voice's encompassing darkness, a ray of light charged through, a light The Voice could not stop even if It tore down heaven and earth.

A light that brought the blackness crashing down in its wake.

A light with a bark, but no bite.

Kaitlyn didn't dream...or maybe she did. She was having difficulty remembering anything before the stifling darkness surrounding her.

Empty darkness.

Deafening silence.

Madness.

An inescapable chasm of nothingness.

She tried to recall how she'd arrived here but came up blank. Something stirred somewhere inside her: a memory.

She chased it, grasped at it with fervor, but it skittered away further into the void.

She was ice cold. She couldn't move her physical body either. She was a statue, paralyzed by the harshness of winter and at the mercy of its crystalline teeth.

The inky shadows were shifting and churning, as if someone–or something–were stirring them.

Indistinguishable shapes emerged, melting into the blackness only to materialize in a different form.

Prickles of unease crackled along the back of her neck, flitting down the gentle curve of her spine.

'*Where am I?*' she thought hesitantly, not entirely sure she wanted to know the answer.

There was another spark of...*something*...far into the recesses that she couldn't quite recollect. She reached out with her mind this time, more slowly than before, more tentative, treating this memory as if it were a skittish, wild animal.

No sooner had she snatched it up, did her world explode in a flash of blinding white light. She was uncertain how long it took for the bright spots to fade from her vision, but when they did, she saw a dark, hazy shape silhouetted against pure white. It was a girl–a woman–with a willowy form and sharp-angled shoulders.

The shape became more distinct, and Kaitlyn instantly recognized the figure of her mom with her flowy fawn colored hair, expressive blue-green eyes, and kind face. Her mom's mouth was moving fluidly, as if she were singing, but Kaitlyn heard nothing, and she didn't care.

Her face lit up as she cried with joy, "Mom!"

At the same moment as someone else.

Brows furrowing, Kaitlyn whipped her head in the direction the second voice came from and saw...

...her. She was looking at an image of herself running toward her mom and into the woman's arms. Saw the slow spread of her mom's malevolent smile as it stretched unnaturally wide across her face, splitting it in half.

It was revolting.

At first Kaitlyn tried to move, to pick up her feet and recoil, but they were stuck. Glued to the illusion of a floor in a place she wasn't certain was real.

She watched in abject horror as the second Kaitlyn was scooped up in her mom's arms, only to have everything shatter with an ear-splitting shriek.

The real Kaitlyn gaped as her mom fell away, then watched her other self-plunge into the black chasm she herself had just come from, screams resounding through the thick air. A cacophonous roar came from the depths of the darkness, followed by the screams of all those before her.

As suddenly as the onset of chaos had come, it stopped, leaving the Dark and Light world hushed once more.

She couldn't muster up the energy to scream, her voice having fallen away into the void after her mom and other self, swallowed by the endless stream of voices.

The first–the original–Kaitlyn stood there in the white

place, mouth agape, eyes nearly bulging from her head, gaping at the towering wall of writhing black looming before her.

She heard an all too familiar sinister cackle reverberate from that blackness, felt the victory and triumphant zeal that oozed from the mocking sound. She could sense it goading and jeering at her, rubbing in her face that she'd lost.

Her small, frail body began to shake.

Cold, callous dread crashed into her being with the force of a speeding truck.

She was convulsing now, feeling as if all her blood was about to rupture through her skin. She slammed her hands over her ears, trying in vain to block out the laughter while possibly attempting to prevent her skull from imploding with the rest of her body. But It got in, It always got in! She felt her mind come unhinged, felt the screws burst from what was supposed to be their permanent homes. Felt everything collapse into nothing.

Nothing.

Nothing...

She fractured, suffered through the agony of her skin cracking inch by inch.

There was nothing she could do about it...powerless, that's what she was.

Powerless.

Weak.

Just like The Scratchy Voice said.

Her voice returned then, surging up through her gut and painfully forcing its way out of her throat in a sound of pure anguish.

It was the sound of a soul shattering. The sound a person made when everything they had ever known was forcefully wrenched away from them.

And it rang out and out and out, echoing through the abyss. The essences in The Darkness ached for her. All the other children, victims of The Voice, reached out to her, but they were too lost amidst the boundless shadows of infinite gloom. They were fragments of who they once were, echoes of a past life that held no power. They were devoured by time, forgotten inside eternity, and no one ever found them, no one ever remembered. Was Kaitlyn destined to suffer this fate as well?

Her fragments fell.

And fell.

...and fell.

Until she was abruptly jerked to a halt.

She was hovering above a sleeping girl.

Above herself in the tent.

Her pale, lifeless form lay pitifully curled in on itself, still as death.

No breath, not even a twitch.

Just silence.

The floating Kaitlyn tried to shout, to reach down and shake her own form.

But she couldn't move, her mouth wouldn't make a sound. She was as frozen as the body below her. The air suspended in her frigid lungs, poised to take a breath that never came.

Kaitlyn's small world, which currently did not reach beyond the small tent, was deathly quiet. Eerie in the most unnatural way.

The floating Kaitlyn allowed the sobs to wrack her body and the tears to waterfall down her face, but all was muted. Her pain was smothered. She had betrayed herself, her own trust that she could–*would*–make it. She didn't deserve to have her emotions vocalized, not when she'd let *It* win. This must've been her punishment, to see for herself what she'd let happen, to see how feeble she really was. She wanted to believe that it was some kind of cruel joke, but even as she attempted to will her thoughts to err on the side of truth, she knew they weren't, would never be. Her situation was very much real, and she couldn't reverse time to fix her mistake.

Too preoccupied with her own grief, she never heard the fast approach of muffled paw steps through the snow nor heard the sound of the soft brush of the nylon flap of the tent being nosed aside. Was not aware of anything aside from the dampness of her cheeks and the quaking of her phantom shoulders.

At least, not until she was suddenly yanked down by an invisible force and thrust back into her body before she could blink.

The murky darkness enveloped her once again, but she didn't panic. What else did she have to lose? She was dead.

Dead.

She was a fool to believe that the odds were ever leaning in her favor at cheating that word.

Dead.

She was dead.

Soon The Voice would come and exult Its victory in her face before happily devouring her essence and discarding her to where all the other children had gone. No one would ever know what happened to her.

Dead.

All because she'd fallen asleep.

She was dead.

All because she failed at the one thing she couldn't afford to do. She'd gambled away money she didn't have without a back-up plan.

Dead.

All because she couldn't fight The Dark, couldn't be as strong as she was supposed to be–

'Stupid! Stupid! Stupid! Weak! What would my parents say? Or Lilly? Oh god...mom...dad...Lilly...no one will find me....no one–'

She instantly became aware of the cold seeping in from all directions, how stiff her limbs were, how painful it was to breathe–

'Wait, did that mean–'

She felt something cold and wet prod at her cheek followed by the overwhelming urge to wipe it away. Her muscles refused to cooperate, however.

She was frozen.

But not dead.

Not yet.

She wasn't dead, she could feel herself breathing.

She wanted to scream and shout and cry with relief, but she still couldn't move. Her body wasn't listening to her, still ensnared in The Voice's Darkness.

She felt the prod again, this time followed by a low whine.

The sound reminded Kaitlyn of when her cream-colored Chow-Chow puppy at home would want food. His name was... Teddy...Teddy! How could she have forgotten about him?

He had only been part of the family for a few months before the start of the 'camping trip,' and she'd had more important things to worry about, so she cut herself some slack.

For now.

Her physical body persisted in its unresponsive state, even as she felt a series of urgent nudges along her side and a shrill bark right in her ear. She wished she could have slammed her hand over her most likely shattered eardrum. She attempted to open her eyes, but they, too, would not listen to the sluggish firings of her brain.

Despite having more than enough reasons, Kaitlyn wasn't afraid. Her mind felt calm, trickling along at the pace of a lazy river. Whatever was there with her, it wasn't dangerous, of that she was certain. It was this knowledge that allowed her consciousness to clear, the screws drifting back to where they belonged, full sensation returning to her as she lay in her sleeping bag. Her panic subsided, even as she remained engulfed in the vast black nothingness.

Something warm and slightly rough suddenly dragged gently over her closed eyelids, the damp thing that felt suspiciously like a tongue lapping specifically along her lash line.

Once again, she attempted to open her eyes, a noise of surprise bubbling up in the back of her throat when she succeeded. She furiously scrubbed at them with the heels of her palms, trying to do away with the unbearable itchiness that seemed to emit from behind her retinas, all the while wiping away the slobber. She was grateful, seeing as said slobber helped her open her eyes, but she still found herself cringing.

'*Gross...*'.

When the intense pain in her eyes subsided to moderately tolerable, she removed her hands and blinked rapidly for a few seconds to reset her blurry vision to the surrounding brightness. She slowly sat up, moving at the typical pace of an elderly woman. The simple gesture was a near impossible task; everything was stiff with fatigue and the everlasting cold that had seeped deep into her bones.

But she managed. When she was fully upright, she rubbed her eyes again to confirm what she was seeing was truly there.

Before her stood a massive black wolf, looming and fierce. It had narrow eyes of a familiar baby blue (she just couldn't remember why it was so familiar). Its fur was unkempt and matted in a few places, but it mostly gleaned in the weak morning light and appeared soft to the touch.

Her first instinct was to flinch away and get as far away from the thing as possible, but the beast didn't look rabid or feral. There was a keen intelligence in its bright gaze that made Kaitlyn wonder if there was more that lay below the surface of this creature.

It was that very intelligence that led Kaitlyn to believe that this wolf would not harm her. She slowly lowered her hackles as the beast moved forward a few steps. It gave Kaitlyn's rib a firm yet interestingly tender nudge, turned around, plopped down on its haunches with a slight huff, proceeding to crane its neck over its broad, strong shoulders, and give a sonorous bark.

Kaitlyn managed to get as far as her knees before she realized she couldn't hardly feel her arms or legs, just a dull stinging where there should have been sensation.

She lifted her fingers in front of her face...they were blue, closer to purple near the tips. She had no doubt her feet were in a similar predicament.

Pushing what the discoloration might mean from her mind, she dragged herself to her swollen feet, but the second she was standing, she crumpled back onto the ground with a barely restrained yelp of pain.

She refused to look down at her feet, to let the panic and despair consume her again. She vowed to not shed any more tears as she curled back into a ball on her side at the top of her sleeping bag.

She didn't want to give up, but she was so tired, so cold and numb. She couldn't even stand or remember why or what she was fighting in the first place. Her eyelids fluttered once, twice.

She might not have been dead yet, but she was going to be.

It wouldn't be long now.

The thought really should have scared her.

The wolf flipped back around to face Kaitlyn, giving a whimper on her behalf.

The thin, papery sound of The Voice buzzed out from the frosty air, sounding abnormally weak, yet not lacking in scorn. Dare it be said that The Voice may have been more than a little enraged, even as it resorted to mockery.

"Just leave her you filthy mutt! Frostbite's already sunk in its teeth. You're too late, I've already won. It won't be long now."

The wolf gave a vicious snarl, hackles rising high. It started barking and growling ferociously toward the opening in the tent, spittle flying, serrated canines flashing with murderous intent at something no living human would ever have the capacity to see.

It was with those words that Kaitlyn fully comprehended what had happened. Where the grogginess had fully evaporated, a sharp awareness took its place; she wanted to scream, she wanted to rip something to shreds.

The Voice had gotten her! She fell asleep and It snatched up her consciousness. It was all coming back to her now. The dream of her mom, The Darkness, the second her, falling...it was all The Voice. It was the one responsible for everything, for manipulating her mind to see those images. She'd let It win.

She'd let It win.

If it hadn't been for the wolf in front of her, she would've been as good as dead. She might still die regardless, and to think she was about to just sit back and let it happen!

'I gave up! Dang it! I had one job, and I couldn't even do that right! Stupid, stupid, stupid! Weak, useless, Kaitlyn!'

But never again.

She pushed herself to her knees.

It would *never* get her again.

She placed one bare, bloated foot on the floor of the tent.

The sound of grinding teeth filled her ears. The wolf was still barking.

She managed to stumble onto her feet, swaying precariously as she took a step.

Another.

And another.

She staggered, watching the world spin around her, as the wolf seemed to double and then triple in her swimming vision.

She took another step.

Blackness hovered teasingly on the outskirts of her vision. She could feel it spreading.

Another step.

She collapsed forward uncontrollably, miraculously falling against the wolf's midnight flank.

The wolf's barking and snarling immediately ceased. It swung its head around to glance at Kaitlyn sagged against its side.

The creature gave her cheek a brisk lick and lowered to a sphinx position.

When Kaitlyn made no move to further climb on, the wolf woofed softly at her.

Pulling up what little strength she had left, Kaitlyn managed to coerce herself into a lying arrangement on the back of the beast, letting out a huff at the effort it took to do such a menial task.

As soon as Kaitlyn was settled, the wolf eased to a kneel

and gingerly stood straight. Kaitlyn draped her arms around its neck and felt a leg slip limply on each side of the wolf's lithe torso.

The beast darted out of the tent and charged into the dead forest. It made no sound as its paws hit the frozen earth, running as if it were a ghost.

Kaitlyn couldn't care less where the creature was taking her, nor did she care about how it was going to get there in this dumb loop forest.

The only thing she could think about was how close she'd been to knocking on death's door, one she may still find herself in front of, if she didn't find a way to get warm soon...she still couldn't believe she'd stopped fighting. That she gave in and let herself be broken down.

Broken.

She promised herself she would never give in.

Crack.

She broke that promise.

With a jolt she realized her cheeks were wet as the silken fur of the wolf's neck stuck uncomfortably to her skin.

'I'm...crying.'

Hadn't she promised she wouldn't cry anymore?

Cra-ck.

Another broken promise.

Another batch of empty words.

She buried her face into the nape of the racing creature, as if she could find some sort of blissful reprieve from her own suffocating thoughts and guilt within the velvety fur. Only she couldn't escape, not from herself, not from The Voice, not from anyone.

That was the thing about these woods, they stripped away a person's ability to suppress what they didn't want to accept.

Her hands fisted into the wolf's silky fur as she burrowed deeper, squeezing her eyes shut until they hurt. She wondered if she would make it—if she even wanted to.

What had she done to deserve being left out in the wilderness by the very same people who were supposed to never do such a thing?

She couldn't remember what any of their voices sounded like, no matter how hard she tried to jog her memory.

She wanted to blame it on her current state, that she simply wasn't in the optimal condition to recall something like that. But it was an issue she'd been having for a while now, except for her mom's lullaby, but that would soon dissolve too. She could already feel the inevitable commencement. Even the images of them were slowly turning fuzzy.

That was another thing about these woods: they made you forget the things you wanted to remember the most.

Her tears came faster, hit full force with the notion that nothing was within her reach anymore, slipping away through the cracks of her fragmented soul. She sought to make it all go away, to refrain from facing the pain more than she had to. All the actions and words and smiles she once thought were genuine, everything that was supposed to be real.

She wanted it to be a nightmare. She wanted to wake up on the couch and see the beautifully decorated Christmas tree with its colorful lights, her sister lounging on the window seat texting one of her mean friends, her mom wrapped up in a fluffy blanket on the recliner reading a book by the fire, her dad sitting at his desk in the corner drinking a cup of coffee while he typed away at his laptop, and sweet little Teddy dozing in his fluffy dog bed in the corner.

She wanted to wake up and see that everything was okay.

She knew that wouldn't happen, though. Her reality was blatantly staring her in the face. A nightmarish one that would never let her go without a fight.

The Darkness gave a heaving push that nearly sent her conscience careening into oblivion. She was grasping on to the pale winter light by a thread as she heard a high-pitched whistle snake its way through the barren trees, the branches creaking and moaning.

The wind caught in her greasy, matted hair and glided over the shell of her ear. She had a fleeting thought of how strange it was that The Voice hadn't spoken since the wolf came into the tent.

Wait.

As the wind continued to tickle her ear she heard the whistle again, long and shrill as it rammed itself right into her eardrum.

She wanted to slam her hands down over her ears until either the insufferable noise ceased its merciless barrage, or she went blissfully deaf, but there was something oddly familiar about that whistle.

Something stirred inside her.

She knew she'd heard it before.

It was mid-November, the weather crisp and chill, though not entirely unbearable yet. Kaitlyn could still go about her day with relative normality.

She was meandering by the hidden stream, scoping out the nearly dead bushes on the slim chance there were still some berries left.

She found herself jumping a mile high when The Voice's uncharacteristically booming voice shattered the virtual silence.

"You won't make it brat. Those before you perished **from frostbite, if they miraculously managed to make it past the first snowfall. You are a pitiful little girl without an inkling on how reality functions. The world would have devoured you. I was right to send those weak-minded** *fools you call family away."*

After recovering from the initial shock of hearing The Voice so suddenly, Kaitlyn froze, fingers instinctually curling into fists. She'd suspected for a while now that The Voice had played a role in her abandonment, but having it directly confirmed made her blood spit and boil in her veins.

"What did you do to them?" she demanded as she glared up at the trees, unsure where else to direct her anger.

She tried to ignore the slight tremor in her words.

"Oh, you know~"

A piercing whistle rang out, loud and chilling. Dreadfully annoying as it continued for what felt like minutes. Maddening.

Having already blocked her ears with the heel of her palms and lacking the patience to handle much more exposure to the unbearable sound, Kaitlyn snapped, "Would you cut it out!"

The whistle ceased immediately and Kaitlyn's shoulders sagged with relief as she let out a breath. Only the earlier silence remained, until it was replaced by the tantalizing lilt of The Voice as It continued.

"...a little that, a little this~~and poof! Gone from **their minds you were, as if you were never there at all. It was simple really, something I picked up centuries ago. An everyday frequency tweaked just-so and the weak-minded** listen to whatever you wish to tell."

Kaitlyn's eyes grew wider the longer she listened. Each word seemed to stab into her body as it was spoken. She was stiff as a ramrod, letting the blunt edge of the truth batter her into the ground like a nail into concrete.

'It can't be. I had a feeling The Voice had done something, but this? This–I...it just can't be. I–I can't be...gone from their minds! I can't!'

She shook her head sporadically, slammed her hands over her ears, her eyes squeezing shut as the thoughts kept coming until she was overflowing with them from the torrential downpour.

"What is it brat? Too much? Can your puny, weak

little human mind not handle the real *truth? Are you going to cry? You are rather exceptional at crying about things you are incapable of changing."*

"Just shut up! You're lying! It's not true! It's not *true!* They wouldn't forget me just because you told them to! They wouldn't! I don't believe you! It's not true!" *were the words that came bellowing out of her mouth as she shook from the arrant rage that raced through her veins.*

There was a smug sounding 'hmm~' before The Voice spoke again.

"If it **is not true, then why are you still** here... alone?"

Kaitlyn stopped shaking. She released the pressure of her hands on her ears, her glaring eyes softening with the rest of her face, the creases between her eyebrows easing away like the tide recedes from the beach. She was overcome with an immense feeling of serene calm. Her blood was no longer boiling, her mind completely clear for the first time in days. She couldn't really describe it. She hadn't an inkling where it came from or why it took control over her so suddenly, but she was glad for it. It seemed purposeful in its appearance inside her.

"If your parents remembered you, surely they would **have collected you** by now," *The Voice finished.*

Kaitlyn strolled quietly toward the transient barrier of the survival spot, a tranquil air about her. The moment before she was about to cross through, she turned around to face the stream once more.

She lifted her chin, her eyes level, her face set in stoic ease.

"You know what Scratchy Voice, it doesn't matter. You don't matter. Whether you're telling the truth or not, I don't care. I'll make it out of these woods, no matter what happens. Maybe I'll have nothing, but at least I'll be away from you. At least I'll be free."

With her parting words, Kaitlyn stepped through the veil and out of the survival spot. Her entire trek back to the clearing, she never looked back.

The Voice didn't bother her for the rest of the day.

Or the next.

Or the next.

Kaitlyn gasped, sitting up straight on the back of the beast, ignoring the painful creaks of her stiffened joints as she did so.

The whistle no longer sang.

It was The Voice's fault. Not hers. She'd done nothing wrong. How could she have forgotten?

How could she have let herself give in after all she'd said?

If only The Voice hadn't made her family forget, if only The Voice hadn't done a lot of things.

What she couldn't fathom was why her family wasn't able to resist The Voice-the whistle-when she could? Was it really because they were older? She knew they loved her, knew they at least cared about her. So how could she have been winked out of their lives so easily? What about the pictures of them on the fireplace mantel or on the wall leading up the stairs? Did The Voice erase those, too? What about her room? Could The Voice really have taken every aspect of her out of her home? What about her dog? He hadn't come with them to go camping, so shouldn't he remember her?

Even if he didn't, Kaitlyn reabsorbed the words she'd spoken all those weeks ago anyway. She held them tight to her chest and swore to never allow them to escape her a second time. They were a reminder that there was a chance. There was a chance that her dog remembered her, which meant he could help her family remember.

The fire inside Kaitlyn raged with a burning determination once again. She was renewed, and in this brief moment of young radiance on the back of a gentle giant, The Voice, nor the cold, could touch her. She vowed to be strong, if not for her family, then for herself.

With a smile on her face, the first smile in months, she laid her head back down on the neck of the beast.

The wind's frigid teeth nipped at her skin, igniting shivers in its wake. Her teeth chattered loudly as she tried to simultaneously hold on to the creature and wrap her arms around herself

The wolf barked deeply, casting a glance over its shoulder, its striking eyes flashing.

By this point her teeth were chattering so fiercely she could no longer speak, so instead she took her trembling hand and gave the wolf a gentle pat between its tapered ears.

Her eyelids fluttered as the blackness crept along the edges of her peripheral, but she willed them to stay open, a single word floating insistently through her head.

'Hurry.'

DAY 136:
A LIGHT TO CALL HOME

A black beast as dark as the night charged through the frozen woods, suspended in a time of ice and death. The body of a small child lay atop its rippling muscles, narrowly hanging on by a thread to a world that was spiraling toward an unforeseeable future.

She may have been safe for now, but becoming too comfortable in that sentiment could be fatal. The wolf was headed toward another survival spot that its pack had claimed as their home. If this forest could be considered a home.

The bitter wind tore at the midnight fur of the creature as it hurled over the ground, kicking up leaves and detritus that transformed into mini whirlwinds as the air currents caught them. But the wolf did not feel the chill. The youth on its back was shivering uncontrollably and mumbling to herself in a way that suggested she was not entirely there. Her eyes were closed, but her eyelids twitched and occasionally flicked up slightly to reveal milky white, eyes rolling sporadically inside their sockets.

There was a battle inside her head, a war that raged between the demons that had been reaped and sewn there.

Recently they seemed to have doubled in numbers and strength, while she seemed to have lost half of her everything. There didn't appear to be an end in sight, yet it never occurred to her to give up. While her intensity wavered at times, its presence remained constant. It was her wildfire, one that brazenly spread the chaos of its inferno.

Perhaps there were wild ones that roamed the world under the mask of civilized humanity. Perhaps society mercilessly beat their fierce spirits into unyielding submission, and they were all merely biding their time until the next moment they'd be able to break free, no longer forced to endure the harsh words or judgmental stares.

Perhaps Kaitlyn was one of them.

Only one person would ever know the answer.

And she was battling all things dark and unseen. The monsters, the demons in her head, the whispers of horrific truths and contorted lies.

She was fading and her flame was dying; she was trapped within her own head with no means of escape.

The wolf thundered across the frozen earth with its large paws, breezing past the branches tearing at its fur. It registered the minor spasms of the girl, the shallowness of her breathing, and unconsciously sped up its already swift pace.

<div align="center">~~~~~~~~~</div>

Kaitlyn stirred awake to the sensation that was similar to walking through a wall of water. Logically, she knew it had only been minutes since the wolf took her away from the clearing, but it felt like hours had passed.

Her eyelids felt cemented shut, her bones aching and creaking as she determinedly tried to sit up. She eventually managed to pry her eyes open to take a look at her surroundings.

The world was a blur, indistinct blobs of color being the only details she could decipher–a light gray patch off to the left, a dark brown to the right, a big blotch of blue straight ahead. She heard what she thought to be the deafening roar of a waterfall. It reminded her of the time her mom took Lilly and her to Niagara Falls. The memory brought a small, fond smile to her face, but it soon fell like the fleeing of a skittish ghost.

The wind picked up again, billowing Kaitlyn's tangled mess of hair. She shivered, but caught a clear, earthy scent on the air currents. The space felt open and wide, as if there wasn't much occupying the current vicinity. Though she wasn't able to put too much more thought to it as she was plunged into shadow, the light fading at her back. She whimpered softly, half expecting to hear The Voice whisper in her ear, but all she was met with was muted silence and the faint echo of the wind still blowing in the distance.

The wolf abruptly kneeled to the ground, 'woofing' gently.

Assuming that was a polite way of saying 'get off,' Kaitlyn dragged herself from its back and collapsed onto her side on the densely packed dirt floor. Everything still felt so cold.

Suddenly there was a fluffy warmth at her back, and one curled around her feet, and another at her head. It wasn't long before she was surrounded by the bodies of an entire pack of wolves. After some time, her joints eased from their frozen stiffness and sensation returned to her hands and feet.

She yawned loudly and snuggled into the fur, feeling the safest she had in the last few months. She sensed no hostility from the wolves, just a fierce protection that felt like being the youngest in the family.

Inexplicably, she was overwhelmed with the feeling that she was going to be okay, no matter what lay beyond the horizon. She knew nothing could touch her here, in a circle of friendly giants. Not the cold, not The Voice, not anything. She was going to live, and she was going to make sure it remained that way. The only difference was now, she no longer had to fight the battle alone.

She secretly hoped The Voice could see her now, how powerless Its words had become. At last, she'd found the antidote to Its poisonous tongue.

Perhaps It had almost beaten her past the point of recovery. But she had reinforcements now, the strength of one now amplified by the strength of many.

CHAPTER FOUR
DAY 1 WITH THE WOLVES: RECOVER

Kaitlyn was encased in darkness the first time she woke up. For a moment, she flailed wildly, shooting into an upright position certain she was back in that horrible shadow place and everything she remembered was but a cruel dream conjured by the ideals of her subconscious, but when she felt the soft brush of fur shift next to her, she relaxed, slowly lying back down. She soon realized this darkness was not like before, gave a content, surprised hum when she found comfort where fear had previously dwelled. This darkness was smooth and velvety, warm and soft, and most of all, safe.

She let her eyes drift closed once more, allowing herself to be lulled back into the welcoming embrace of sleep by the wolves' gentle, wheezing snores.

~~~~~~~~~~

Kaitlyn was jostled awake the second time she woke up. She almost immediately sat up and fisted her eyes to remove the drowsiness. She hadn't slept that well in months, despite not sleeping for the whole night, she realized with a start that sent her eyes flying open. With that she soon discerned why and what had woken her up: moonlight was streaming into the cave in streaks of glittering silver, glinting off the wolves' shiny coats as they huddled at the cave opening. A gust of wind blew through the mouth of the cave, leading Kaitlyn to curl
~~~~~~~~~~

into herself and scoot deeper into the open space. The cold triggered something deep in her brain and she instinctively looked down at her hands and feet, only to heave a great sigh of relief as she found their normal coloring had returned. The only remaining evidence at their previous state was that her fingers and toes were slightly red from leftover inflammation.

She diverted her attention back to the front of the cave as three wolves separated from the pack and trotted over to her, settling themselves around her. Two of them appeared slightly frail underneath their lean muscles, as if their youth was fading. The other one was disheveled, fur tangled and matted in some places. Kaitlyn smiled at them, though she suspected they didn't comprehend it.

She glanced back to the rest of the wolves, the big black one that saved her at the head of the pack, obviously the leader. The wolf suddenly bounded over to Kaitlyn in an almost playful manner before giving her a fond lick on the forehead and racing back to the cave mouth and out into the night. The rest of the pack followed at its heels, leaving Kaitlyn sitting there with only the other three wolves to keep her company.

Now that she thought about it, surrounded by wolves, she didn't think she looked that out of place. She was tattered and dirty and just as unkempt. She suspected her appearance wasn't particularly different from that of a wild animal.

Alone in the soft, wispy shadows of the cave, she was more than a little apprehensive that The Voice would make a reappearance and begin taunting her like It did every morning, but her worries never became reality. The remaining wolves' gentle breathing served as a comforting sound that put her at ease. The near silence felt refreshing. And if the wolves were with her, she knew she was safe. She reveled in the new, tentative peace that befell her world.

She allowed her body to relax, her shoulders sagging and the lines on her face softening. She scooted until she was lodged in the corner at the very back of the cave. The internal space curved slightly to the right, so Kaitlyn's position gave her protection from any stray drafts that would happen to loft in.

The other three wolves huddled in closer, mimicking her movement. One was pressed against her outstretched leg, his fur a mousy brown with a silver dusting around his muzzle and down his spine. His blue-gray eyes reminded Kaitlyn of the ocean right before a storm.

Another was curled around Kaitlyn's feet, her fur a creamy white and eyes a pretty, pale gold.

The other wolf was outstretched against the dark, rocky wall beside Kaitlyn. He appeared to be the smallest of the three, his fur entirely gray mixed with varying shades of brown. His eyes, a piercing silver, were in stark contrast with his shaggy fur.

Moments later Kaitlyn had dozed off again with the thought *'I wonder where the other wolves went,'* drifting lazily down her stream of consciousness.

She didn't know how long she was out, but she awoke when a beam of bright sunlight fell upon her, casting her face in deep orange shadows. She squinted into the light, holding her hand up to block the majority of it, only to have the sun obstructed entirely as a dozen or so furry silhouettes shuffled into the cave.

The black wolf, that Kaitlyn decided to identify as Midnight to make things easier on herself, dragged something limp through the pack and refused to be hindered until she was in front of Kaitlyn. Kaitlyn had a brief glimpse to realize that it was a deer before two of the wolves who had kept her company lunged and started to tear savagely into the flesh. Movement from the corner of her eye told her the smaller one had dashed out of the cave.

She watched with rapt attention as the meat disappeared before her eyes. She was surprised to find she wasn't outright repulsed, even when the blood oozed and sprayed, and the innards spilled out onto the packed floor.

Had this been under any other circumstance, she probably would have thrown up.

She briefly wondered where the wolves had found a deer when she struggled to find a measly squirrel. The thought caused her to look up at Midnight, who was seated a few feet away, watching Kaitlyn watch her.

There was a strange look in the beast's peculiar blue eyes, one Kaitlyn couldn't decipher before the wolf turned and trotted back to the cave's entrance.

She soon returned with something dangling from her jaws, setting down what Kaitlyn realized to be a white rabbit. Its throat was bitten and torn, likely the killing blow. She found herself a little upset at the image in front of her, though not upset enough to foolishly turn away the meal.

She gingerly picked up the lifeless form before the other wolves could snatch it and stood.

"I'll be back," she said to the black wolf and immediately strode out into the bitter cold.

She shivered as the wind blew fiercely and tore at her tattered nightgown, clutching the rabbit to herself.

The sun, by contrast, as it rose above the naked trees surrounding the clearing, provided a faint warmth as it bathed her face in golden light.

She continued walking until she was at the edge of the lake in the center of the clearing, taking a moment to stare in awe as she gazed up at the waterfall spilling over a short precipice about 10 yards away.

The roar was deafening. She'd heard it in the cave, but up close and at a distance were two very different things. It emitted power, contradicting the delicate mist that hovered over the clear lake surface.

There was a long outcrop of pale rock off to her left, a little shorter than the surrounding trees and scattered with boulders of various sizes, almost resembling a wall. An aged, crumbling wall that had seen the despairing throes of war. The rest of the clearing was surrounded by dead trees, and the ground made of the same packed dirt as the floor of the murky cave behind her. She saw no trace of the other wolf that had departed earlier.

Having finished her inspection of the area, she crouched at the water's edge where it lapped lazily at the tips of her toes, setting the rabbit down beside her. Gazing into the water, she scored what she could see of the lake bed for any rocks she could potentially use to light a fire.

When she spotted none, her gaze gradually slid to the rocky patch off to her left.

Not wanting to stay in the cold any longer than she had to, she shrugged before moving to grab the rabbit. But as she turned, the sun latched onto to something bright and silvery in the water.

It only lasted for a fraction of a second before disappearing. She carefully moved her head until the light caught on the unknown object again. It was about a yard out in the water.

With her curiosity piqued, she left the rabbit where it was and adjusted her head until the object was no longer shining. With a miniscule quirk of her brow, she saw what appeared to be some sort of blade resting on the lake bed.

'I wonder how that got there....' She thought to herself, thinking it rather odd. She had no reason to believe that others had been here before.

After pondering it a moment longer, she shrugged, about to leave it be since it was too far out for her to reach without getting wet anyway, when it occurred to her that it could prove useful.

She could still dismiss it, but she didn't want to. She whipped her head around, diligently searching the space for anything she could potentially use. Perhaps a stick, a *very long* stick.

An idea suddenly popped into her head that had her sprinting off toward the rocks to her left and scrambling up the slope, dust and gravel cascading down in her wake. When she reached the top, she mindfully made her way to the edge where the spidery fingertips of some branches were grazing the crumbling stone. As she drew closer, she realized how abruptly the rock fell away. She reeled back a step as a sheer drop of 50 feet glared up at her from between the branches.

She gulped, lowering to her knees and slowly inching forward. She understood she was being incredibly stupid at this moment and began to wonder why she thought this was a good idea.

She firmly grasped a branch as far down as she could reach without hanging half her body over the edge. She inched forward a bit further...and some of the rock collapsed beneath her knee.

She lost her balance.

She started to fall.

Everything seemed to progress in slow motion.

She squeezed her eyes shut so tight she saw flashes of color streak madly across the darkness behind her eyelids.

She felt herself falling and held on to the branch for dear life, praying to whatever deity that might be listening that it would hold.

It did. Barely.

She flicked her eyes open, the world swimming for a moment, bright spots bursting intermittently across her vision, her heart nearly hammering a hole through her chest. When she happened to look down, she found herself suspended over airy nothingness, the ground seeming much farther down than she'd originally anticipated. The ground seemed to pulse, almost taunting her, though she suspected that was just the dizziness taking its effect.

When the wind gave a powerful blast of wintry air, she realized the extent at which the branch she was clinging to had had begun to bow from her insubstantial weight. She was quick to shimmy forward until she sat on a thicker, sturdier part of the branch.

After resting for a moment to calm her racing heart, she meticulously descended through the boughs and down the tree, only stopping long enough to snag a branch she deemed an appropriate length before continuing her descent to the ground. When her feet touched solid earth, she sank to her knees, collapsing back on the thick bole of the tree. Her heart thudding hard in her chest, her blood racing in her ears, her body shaking like a leaf. She'd come an inch from knocking on death's door...again. She found herself cackling, discovering an absurd hilarity in the situation. Somehow escaping death once had her numb for the second time, possibly knocking another screw loose in her already flimsy sanity. She quickly sobered though, realizing she had to let go of this 'I'm invincible because I'm young' mindset if she wanted to make it through, at the very least, another day.

Upon the reappearance of the icy breeze, she hopped up, grabbed her stick that she just had to have, and whisked out from behind the rock and over to the lakeshore where her rabbit remained limp and lifeless. She crouched at the edge of the water, the blade glinting wickedly, and extended the branch over the clear blue lake until it extended slightly past the object.

She dipped the thick end of the stick into the water, proceeding to nudge the blade closer to the shore.

It wasn't long before she was awkwardly clutching the slick handle of a small hunting knife, no sign of oxidation having occurred. She stared, astounded. It looked brand new, the only indication at its age being the weathered wood of the handle, which could have easily just been from the time spent in the water.

She glanced around, she'd never been allowed to touch the knives at home, so in a way, holding this thing made her nervous. She half expected to hear her mom's scolding tone from behind her. She gave an indignant 'hrumph' and began to turn the knife over in her hand, scrutinizing it as if to show that her mom's rules no longer applied to her.

She deposited it beside the rabbit before heading to the stone, wall-like structure and diligently selected two medium sized chunks of Jasper and as many twigs and leaves as she could carry. A few moments later, she had a happily crackling fire, thin wisps of gray smoke wafting up toward the heavens. She glanced back down at the knife. Almost instinctively, she picked up the rabbit and the blade and clumsily began skinning the animal. Her dad once took her on a hunting trip with him and let her watch him skin a deer afterward, so she had some idea of what to do, but lacked the finesse to carry out the task neatly. She tried to keep her flinches to a minimum, and when she was finished, she took a medium sized stick she'd retrieved earlier and skewered it through the rabbit meat. While it should have concerned her that she wasn't sickened by any of this like she was when she'd watched her dad, she just couldn't bring herself to care. She wondered how her past self would react if she could see herself now.

She cast aside those thoughts, not wanting to dwell on things she didn't have answers for, nor wanted the answers to.

She began the rather tedious process of roasting the rabbit, occasionally turning the stick so it cooked evenly. She'd made the mistake of not turning it before, learned her lesson when she'd brought a new meaning to the word 'crispy.'

She didn't know how long it had taken the meat to cook, but obviously a while if the number of times she saw

Midnight poke her head out of the cave was anything to go by.

She eventually removed the stick from the fire, watching with rapt attention as grease dripped from the steamy, golden flesh. Her stomach rumbled violently.

She allowed the rabbit to cool for as long as she dared before ferociously tearing into it. Grease spewed and her eyes flashed with something feral, a growl resonating deep in her throat. She consumed it in seconds, more animal than man.

Afterwards her inner animal retreated into the depths of her consciousness as the wind gave a ruthless wheeze across the clearing. She hastily wiped her mouth and then her slick hands on the tatters of her nightgown, scooped a handful of dust from the ground in each hand, and tossed it over the dwindling fire so it poofed out. She plucked the bloody rabbit fur and the leftover bones from the ground and ran to the edge of the clearing where she dug a shallow grave for what was left of the creature. When finished, she sped back to the fire, a few embers still glowing, and swiped the knife from where it lay by the remains of the fire. She bolted back into the cave–being mindful of the blade–that she suspected was now her new home.

When she passed through the mouth of the cave, she stored the knife in a little nook she'd noticed a few feet up the stone wall. The pack of wolves huddled near the back; some dozed while others were grooming each other or lounging lazily. Midnight was sitting up and alert as if waiting for Kaitlyn to return. She went and joined them, plopping down near a spot in the back that provided the most shelter from the wind. A few moments later, the smaller wolf she'd seen run out earlier returned, immediately taking up residence on the outskirts of the group.

She thought it would have taken a lot longer to become so comfortable around wild animals. She knew they were dangerous creatures of which humans tried to avoid at all costs. Yet, when Kaitlyn saw Midnight for the first time in her tent, she didn't feel threatened. She didn't receive any indication that told her this was an unpredictable, ruthless killer of a beast. Though it was obvious to her that this wasn't the type of behavior typically associated with a wolf. She wondered why that was, voicing her thoughts aloud to Midnight, who was still sitting upright, staring at Kaitlyn with eyes that held a deep wisdom unfitting of an animal with such notoriety.

The only response Kaitlyn received was a yawn, exposing a mouth full of sharp, slightly yellowed canines before Midnight lay down on the ground as well.

Kaitlyn blinked. She really shouldn't have expected anything different.

With nothing better to do since she wasn't sleepy yet, she restarted her day counting with small sections of twigs like before.

A few minutes later, a thunderstorm seemingly materialized out of thin air, the rain coming down by the buckets. Lightning flashed, illuminating the shadowy world outside with eerie fluorescence. The thunder exploded from the sky with a roaring intensity that held the wrath of a thousand gods. The wind howled through the branches, thrashing them violently to and fro. Despite the ferocity, Kaitlyn found her eyes fluttering closed as she listened to the raging world outside. The tension she didn't know was there left her shoulders, and she basked in the sheer power and chaos of the storm.

She eventually grew restless and began the painful task of attempting to detangle her rat's nest of hair. It, however, quickly became futile as no more than a few strokes in her fingers could not be dragged any further, no matter how hard she tugged. She persisted until she saw a very faint orange hue along the horizon. A frustrated growl left her chapped lips as she abruptly stood, causing

Midnight to quickly lift her head with a confused 'hrum'? Kaitlyn stomped to the front of the cave, hands balled in tiny fists at her sides, grumbling furiously the whole way.

"Stupid hair–good for nothing–can't *believe*–!"

The bitter wind whipped at her viciously as the still pouring rain blew sideways into the cave. She ignored it.

She withdrew the knife from the place she'd stashed it, stepped back out of range of the splashing rain, sat down, and hesitated no more than a millisecond before she started sawing away at her hair.

It flittered to the ground in long, knotty strands. Before long, she was left with a choppy, uneven length that barely brushed her shoulders in some places.

She knew it looked horrendous, but it's not like there was anyone else around to poke fun at it. She tipped backwards and found herself sprawled on her back, limbs splayed like a starfish, practically swimming in a dark sea of criss-crossing labyrinths. She breathed a sigh of relief. It felt so much lighter.

She gazed up at the gray ceiling, watching what little was left of the dull light from outside fade into a gloomy dusk. It was the cold that finally persuaded her to move away from the entrance. She decided to leave the clean-up job for the morning, rather than fumbling around in the dark.

Feeling along the cave wall, she eventually found the cranny she'd stored the knife in. After returning the object, she shuffled through the inky blackness, carefully picking her way over the sleeping bodies scattered across the back of the cave. She settled herself in the rear corner, feeling one of the wolves shift closer to her.

Her own yawn was unexpected as she made herself more comfortable. She still half expected to hear The Scratchy Voice and Its terrible whispers, but similar to the night before, there was no such thing, only the soft patter of the rain to keep the wandering thoughts company. She admitted to herself how strange it was not hearing The Voice throughout the day, though it wasn't unwelcome. She didn't miss trying to stay awake twenty-four-seven nor her nervous-system working over-time. Although, she would have to find an alternative way to maintain her speaking now that the voice was currently out of the picture.

As she drifted off into an untroubled sleep, the thought that she could get used to this way of life came unbidden through the shadows. She succumbed to the drag of exhaustion before her brain could begin to comprehend how alarming that internal sentiment truly was.

CHAPTER FIVE
DAYS 2 AND ONWARD: THROUGH THE DARK

Kaitlyn didn't stir when the wolves departed late that night. She did, however, rouse when the symphony of howls rang sequentially through the forest. The sound rose in volume, causing her to jerk awake so violently that her knee slammed into the cave wall. She yelped, clutching at the throbbing area as the howls continued to travel through the still air. When the tears brimming in her eyes cleared, she managed to crane her head around and see that the rain had ceased at some point during the night, leaving the silver beam from the moon–the *full moon*–to spill into the cave entrance. The view outside was otherworldly; there wasn't a cloud in sight, the clearing basked in a pale sheen, the small lake transformed into liquid mercury. It was ethereal, and it would have made her never want to look away, had it not been so ludicrously bright.

Giving a half-hearted grumble, she buried her head into the crook of her elbow and patiently waited for the howls to subside before seamlessly slipping back into unconsciousness.

She fully awoke a few hours later to another beam of light shining in her face, nearly blinding her in the process. Despite appreciating its warmth, she screwed her face up into a look that can only be described as 'the scrunch face.' Honestly, that whole thing about 'he looked at her like she was the sun' didn't even make any sense, if the way that Kaitlyn so desperately wanted to throttle the sun out of the Milky Way was anything to go by.

She squeezed her eyes shut, proceeding to push herself into an upright position, her bones creaking in protest as she did so. She stretched her arms wide, a series of satisfying pops skittering down her spine. She'd eventually need to retrieve her sleeping bag from the tent if she ever wanted her muscles to stop aching, though even the thought of doing so made her shiver.

She turned toward the source of sunlight and nearly jumped out of her skin as she found Midnight sitting right off to her left, another rabbit dangling from her mouth.

Kaitlyn pursed her lips at the beast, voicing aloud with a disgruntled scowl, "You scared me!"

The wolf set the rabbit down, had the audacity to look apologetic.

Kaitlyn smiled wide at the creature, the corners of her mouth pinching slightly with the foreignness of it.

"It's okay," she eventually said.

The wolf made a soft noise at Kaitlyn before trotting back to the front of the cave where the rest of the wolves were returning. She snatched the rabbit as she saw the three wolves that had stayed with her the day before making their way to the front as well. Once certain they had gone, she headed to the cave entrance herself, wading through the small sea of wolves until she was in the clearing. Though not before seizing the knife. The piercing cold persisted, but the abundance of sunlight took the chill off the air.

She went through the process of skinning and cooking the rabbit, then burying the rabbit skin as she did the previous day. After her meal, she tried her best to even out her hair like she'd seen her mom do to herself after a bad salon experience, using the surface of the lake as a makeshift mirror. Once finished, she concluded her actions with a satisfied nod and returned the knife.

She attempted to clean up the hair from the day before, though it had been scattered by the wind and from the wolves trampling it. It looked like Bigfoot had gone and shed his way through the cave. After a fit of snickers, she gathered what hair she could, then just sat there with it pooling in her lap, staring down at it as if it might jump up and bite her.

Should she keep it? Bury it? What? She had no idea if it could be useful in the future or not. If she did keep it, what would she even use it for? Wouldn't it just break?

'Seems kinda pointless to me. And it'd be weird to keep my own hair, wouldn't it?' she asked herself.

She knew there was no one around to judge her for it, but she couldn't shake the fact that she would feel like a complete weirdo if she kept it. She could still hear what she thought to be her sister's frequently used slogan, "Nobody likes a weirdo," though she couldn't remember the sound of her sister's voice. That realization sent a jolt surging through her chest; she quickly batted it away.

She was beginning to feel itchy, so with her mind made up, she hastily rushed out into the chilly morning to bury the strands next to the rabbits. Soon she was hurrying back into the cave and joining the dozing wolves at the back. Since it was too cold out to do anything of significance, she settled in and began reviewing all the knowledge she'd acquired in her ten years of existence.

She started with what she'd learned in school thus far, but that thought made her freeze. School hadn't so much as crossed her mind until now. Does that mean that The Voice erased her from the minds of her friends and teachers as well? That had to be the case, otherwise people would've come looking for her by now, right? Her chest started heaving. She had to force herself to calm down and fight against the wave of hopelessness that threatened to consume her. It was what The Voice wanted, and that wasn't a liberty she was about to let It have.

'But...how could I be...gone? Just like that? Completely erased from time?'

Her form began to tremble as she realized no one probably knew she existed anymore. She couldn't fathom how it was possible to delete her from the minds of anyone who had ever known her. If that was the case, then Teddy wouldn't remember her either. It would mean no one did.

She mentally chastised herself. *'No! Stop thinking like that! There has to be a way.'*

She nodded firmly to herself, as if the action would manifest her thoughts into reality.

She eventually returned to reviewing information, from what she'd learned in school to what her parents and sister had taught her, to what she'd concluded on her own. She told herself that she'd have to seriously thank her dad for all the things she knew about the wilderness and survival skills if–no, *when* she got out of this forest.

There were some gaps in her memory, facts she struggled to recall or advice she remembered being told but couldn't piece the wording together. Much to her distaste, she had to let go of anything that escaped her before she drove herself mad trying to chase after it. Next, she moved on to recalling the details about her family, and while she was still able to recollect their appearances and mannerisms, she could not recall the sound of their voices anymore.

Catching her unawares, a chord was struck in her as the brunt of that realization smacked her like a ton of bricks. She curled in on herself as her shoulders shook with the ferocity of a silent earthquake. At first, she made not a sound. But then a soft, wounded noise escaped her cracked lips, and the sobs that followed roused the wolves sleeping around her.

She had tried not to think about it, to hold it back from the forefront of her mind, but she couldn't do it anymore. She slumped to the floor of the cave as tears flowed steady down her face. Everything bubbled up in her all at once, and the only place it had left to go was out.

Her fist slammed down onto the hard, packed dirt of the cave. The resulting zing of pain up her arm only made her cry harder. She didn't care. She just wanted to feel something other than the anguish that was in danger of swallowing her whole. Her fist connected with the ground again, and again.

"Why!?" she cried out.

Thump.

"Why me!? What did I ever do?!"

Thump.

"Why me God!? What did I do to deserve this?! Why are you letting this happen?!" She finally managed to voice aloud what she'd been wondering all along.

"How could you let this happen to me?! How could you let them *leave me here*!? Some God you are, you're supposed to look out for everyone! You're just as bad as The Scratchy Voice; you don't care at all!"

Thump.

She released a sound as if someone had punched her in the stomach.

"I just want to go home! I want my family back! I can't even remember what they sound like!" her voice cracked, leading her to fall into a coughing fit that wracked her frail body. The tears refused to cease, and she soon found herself screaming at the cave's murky ceiling.

It ricocheted off the walls, filled the air with its excruciating agony that traveled for miles. Somewhere in the world, lightning struck down a tree. Set it aflame with a fire that burned with the rage of a thousand men. Her chest was burning so ferociously she could hardly breath, felt as if she was being ripped apart by her own grief. She wanted it all to stop. She wanted to go home, she wanted her family, but The Voice had snatched them away from her, and God had let it happen, and there was nothing she would ever be able to do about it. In that moment, the task of getting out of the forest seemed too impossible to comprehend.

She struck the ground again, another scream ripping through the air aimed at the heavens. The wolves sat by idly in silence, letting the events run their natural course. When Kaitlyn's body finally went limp, fist aching and raw, her lip trembling, eyes still trickling tears down her blotchy cheeks as the occasional hiccup shook her, Midnight slowly rose and padded across the short distance between them. She planted herself down beside the child, and Kaitlyn immediately clutched at the wolf's thick coat, burying her face into the softness as if trying to escape the pain.

She fell asleep like that, eventually followed by the rest of the pack. There was no moon that night, for its luminescence was deliberately tucked away behind the blanket of clouds covering the obsidian sky.

She subconsciously relaxed at the arrival of darkness. It tenderly caressed the planes of her skin, exhibiting the touch only a mother could. Wove its way through her hair and gently brushed any remnants of tears away into the night. It settled over her like a velvet blanket as she sank deeper into her slumber.

~~~~~~~~~~

Over the next week, December passed into January, and with it, much to Kaitlyn's dismay, more rain and more snow. She'd had to move the fire inside the cave as an attempt to fend off the dropping temperatures. She woke up, she ate, she added another piece of stick to her pile, and spent the remainder of each day reviewing everything she'd learned in her life. The tears had returned only once that week, though this time the unwilling target of her blame had been her. 'What ifs' and agonizing over things outside of one's control were one of the mind's worst kinds of self-inflicted torture.

The wolves gave her space during her outbursts, showing
~~~~~~~~~~

no indication of apprehension as she grabbed anything she could get her hands on and started hurling the objects in all directions with agony filled wails. The canines never failed to swoop in and clean up the aftermath. Kaitlyn could almost trick herself into believing that it was her family wrapped around her.

She also found herself with more free time that she would prefer since she no longer had to concern herself with hunting. Far too much time to think about when her life had taken a swan dive into an unknown abyss.

She came to understand it was dangerous, thinking too much. Not like she had much choice when it was her only option to pass the time. This led to her recognizing that she had to find some form of balance between who she used to be, and who she had become. And while she'd gotten pretty good at thinking, she didn't allow herself to think too much deeper into it than that.

The nights proved to remain the most difficult, however. While solace, for the most part, had made its way into her soul, a feeling of unease still lurked within its depths. With nightfall came the unforgotten echoes of The Voice. She had to keep reminding herself that The Voice couldn't reach her here, which dispelled some of the ominous association to the blackness that hugged the nooks and crannies around her.

On one abnormally warm, windless night, Kaitlyn found herself gazing into the clearing, the wolves having left for their nightly hunt. She hadn't been able to easily fall asleep that night, and eventually grew irritated with her own tossing and turning.

She allowed her mind to become blank as her eyes scanned the grayscale terrain, a small snow drift obscuring what she could fully see. She sensed the darkness from the cave at her left, how half of her fell in shadow, half of her illuminated by the silvery crescent grin that was suspended in the lucid black sky. There were more stars than she had ever seen in her life; divine fragments of forgotten souls dotted the heavens to the brim. They twirled around this massive rock suspended in infinite space, around the milky clearing, the mercury water and the rippling shadows conversing in the tree line. She imagined she was on another planet, that earth was no more. And she forgot. For a few brief, shining moments, she forgot. And it was glorious. The trees clawing at the sky were wise, old, spiny-haired giants standing guard. She imagined the boulders off to the side coming alive at any moment to start singing in their native tongue, that beautiful creatures fashioned from the moon would surface the water and beckon her closer to tell her the secrets of the universe. The crescent moon would sprout a complimenting set of eyes and spout off jokes that would make her laugh until her stomach hurt. The stars would grow wings, swooping down to take her on a tour of the galaxies.

For a little while, she wasn't lost or frightened or angry. She was a child, and she was happy.

CHAPTER SIX
ALL THIS TIME THAT CAME AND WENT

Over the following three months, Kaitlyn found herself unwillingly falling victim to monotony. Her 11th birthday came and went during the blur of March. She never noticed. She rarely spared acknowledgement toward the wolves anymore. They were lucky if they received a curt nod or a half-hearted grunt.

She found herself almost obsessively sitting at the front of the cave each night, staring out at nothing, lost inside a mind that was slowly caving in on itself. In spite of it all, she always made sure that the wolves knew she appreciated their help.

Most days she secluded herself in the rear of the cave, hunched into the corner and back turned toward the world, nothing but the cool stone walls to keep her company. Her chest pooled with an enduring tightness, the self-inflicted isolation ensuring her waterline remained damp. Her mind screamed at her, but her body stayed limp, imprisoned by the thousand-yard stare. There was no anger, no sadness, no anything, just fluttering eyelids and short-lived escapes into mindless, unconscious oblivion.

She'd become an empty house, rooms abandoned and desolate, dust piled high in the corners and floating in the pale slivers of light that shone through the boards nailed to the cracked windows.

Her ribs became more prominent, hollows formed beneath her cheekbones, her skin sallow and gray tinged, and her nightgown no longer in a state that could be considered clothing.

She gradually began to sleep more into the day, rising later into the night. Though oftentimes she merely rose whenever the sun refused her plea for a reprieve. For those three months, life was unimaginably bleak. At least before the wolves, she had something to focus on, though she wasn't entirely sure if she would rather return to her old clearing with The Voice or not. The wolves had saved her after all. She shouldn't have had to keep reminding herself of that.

'I wonder what death feels like,' she wondered one day.

'It has to be better than this,' she answered herself miserably, then quickly shook her head in rejection. *'No, no, don't think like that.'*

The future was nothing but a dark splotch on the horizon; The thoughts kept coming, no matter how many times she scolded herself for 'thinking like that.' Today was solely an in between of forever accumulating yesterdays and tomorrows that may never come.

Salvation came with a break in the dreary weather, on a night many would consider April Fools.

Kaitlyn awoke to Midnight persistently nosing at her side. She tried to push the wolf away and go back to sleep, but Midnight only pushed with more force. The large beast began gently nipping at Kaitlyn's exposed skin, and when that didn't work, resorted to pulling sharply at Kaitlyn's hair with her teeth.

Sitting up with an outraged cry and a scowl fixed on her face, now fully awake, Kaitlyn glared at the wolf, rubbing her stinging scalp.

"What are you trying to do?" she growled.

Midnight made an affronted noise, moving behind Kaitlyn and nudging her toward the mouth of the cave.

With a suspicious look thrown the wolf's way, Kaitlyn crossed her arms and resigned to begrudgingly letting herself be pushed forward. When she was out of the cave and under the watchful gaze of the moon shrouded in thin wisps of clouds, she expected to be hit with an icy blast of air. Instead, the breeze was verging on bearable. Belatedly, she startled slightly upon noticing that the whole pack was spread before her like a fan.

Kaitlyn's eyebrows quirked upward marginally, side-eying Midnight as if awaiting a verbal explanation from the creature as to why she'd been so rudely awoken and forced out of the cave against her will.

The beast provided no such clarification, efficiently gathering the pack together and advancing toward the tree line at a gentle trot.

Kaitlyn stared after them, a blank look on her face, an expression that had recently taken up permanent residence on her features.

When Midnight realized Kaitlyn wasn't following her, she stopped, looking over her broad shoulder. Meeting Kaitlyn's vacant stare, she barked and waited.

Registering about two dozen pairs of eyes watching her, Kaitlyn took a tense step forward, stiff as a board. She jerked to a stop, praying that Midnight didn't want her to do what she was beginning to suspect she did.

Midnight barked again; this time echoed by other members of the pack.

Kaitlyn shook her head sharply, balling her hands into fists to hide the fact that they were shaking.

Midnight turned around fully, followed by yet another bark, this one louder. It resounded throughout the clearing, fracturing the tranquil silence.

Kaitlyn shook her head again, more forcefully this time, a muscle ticking minutely in her jaw. She felt her chipped nails dig into the soft flesh of her palms.

Midnight parted from the pack and padded her way over to Kaitlyn. She tenderly bumped her nose into Kaitlyn's hip before whining up at her.

Kaitlyn bit her lip, feeling the whirlwind of emotions bubble to the surface after having been numb for so long.

She found herself unsteady on her feet, chest growing tight as it felt like her windpipe had swelled to double its size. Her eyes frantically darted back and forth, a bead of sweat trickling down the back of her neck.

She ran a hand through her hair as she gazed into the forest, the shadows writhing amid the dark trunks, just out of reach of the rays of moonshine that shone between the mostly barren tree branches. She somehow knew they were waiting for her, more importantly, that The Voice was waiting for her.

Her eyes widened.

She gulped.

She jolted awake out of her senseless oblivion, like she'd been doused with a bucket of ice water and subsequently delivered an electric shock. Flinching, she realized that she had no idea where her mind had gone. All she could recall was a vast, hollow emptiness. She'd been mindless, wandering far away in the sunflower fields in her mind. She found reprieve amongst the tall stems and the gentle flitter of butterfly wings. There had been no pain there, no problems requiring her attention, just peace. And yet, all that time, she could've been scheming her next course of action.

All that time, wasted.

'Perhaps you needed it,' came a voice from inside her head.

'Perhaps you needed to go away for a while,' it finished.

Kaitlyn's eyes widened even further as understanding finally dawned on her, a gentle presence settling into place inside of her. What's done was done, no use in agonizing over it now.

She returned to her current predicament, taking another halting step forward, then stopping again. She was certain she heard unintelligible whispering, dark and ominous, rising and falling in volume and intensity. She suspected she'd seen far too much to chalk it up to her imagination this time.

Clenching her jaw, grinding it back and forth, her hands constricted into fists before softening, fingers flaring out and then curling back in.

The wolves watched patiently.

She closed her eyes, head tilting to the left.

The whispers grew more intense, more deliberate.

She squeezed her eyes shut harder, shifted her neck from side to side, rolled her shoulders.

A long, high-pitched whistle sounded from the churning silvery black that lay beyond the tree line.

Her eyes snapped open, a determined flash of blue-green lightning, and charged into the forest.

When she passed into the loop forest, it was like transcending into another world. She jerked to a stop a few yards into the wood, appearing to have reached the end of her tether. The wolves pooled around her, attempting to form a protective barrier.

Darkness descended over Kaitlyn's skin, the mindless whispers growing louder. She cringed away until she found herself illuminated in a beam of moonlight. While the shadows still clung to her, she was relieved of some of her discomfort. This darkness wasn't the same as what she'd often found comfort in within the wolves' clearing; this darkness...felt wrong. It was all wrong–slimy even, as if it was attempting to slither its way under her skin.

The whispers continued to increase in volume as she stood frozen amid a sea of inky tree silhouettes. They seemed to squirm, to pulsate and shy away from what little light had been afforded.

She slammed the heels of her palms over her ears as the whispers gained volume. Her head shook vehemently, she curled into herself to try and shut out the unbearable noise. The Darkness sloshed around her, growing even louder, and just when she was about to start screaming, the whispers ceased abruptly. The Darkness slipped away from her skin, as if a switch was flipped, leaving the forest unnaturally silent.

The wolves immediately encircled her, pressing directly up against her flanks, many of them emitting throaty growls, deep and menacing, as Kaitlyn gingerly righted herself.

"Well, well, well, look what we have here," The Voice drawled.

Kaitlyn glared up at the skeletal branches above her, assuming that was where The Voice was.

"What do *you* want?" She scoffed.

"Tsk, tsk. Foolish girl," It jeered.

Kaitlyn's hands once again found themselves in fists. "I escaped. Anything to say about that?" she shot back.

*"But you haven't escaped from this place. You **are still here all on your own~. You are no closer to leaving than** you were on day one. Are you incapable of understanding **that there is no hero to your pathetic tale?**"* It hissed.

Her vision flashed red. "You're the reason my family left! It's *your* fault!" she shouted.

"Is that so?" It drawled lowly. *"**It seemed that some time ago you were blaming that deplorable excuse for a god of yours. Do make up your mind child.**"*

She deliberately disregarded the comment.

"Also, I'm not alone. I have the wolves," Kaitlyn said sensibly.

*"A most **unfortunate reality**,"* The Voice sneered.

Kaitlyn rolled her eyes, clenching her jaw yet again. She felt her teeth ache as she did so.

She pointedly turned her back from where she was facing. She'd prove It wrong if it was the last thing she ever did. She directed her attention to Midnight off to her right. The creature seemed to understand because, without warning, she bolted deeper into the murky forest. Kaitlyn began running as well, kicking up dead leaves in her wake. The rags of what used to be a nightgown flapped around her legs, her short, untamed hair flying as the warm breeze dragged its fingers through it. She was vaguely aware that The Voice had started talking again, but Its words were drowned out by the roaring in her ears. Mentally hoping her lack of attention infuriated It.

She realized she was falling behind the pack, so she bore down and pumped her arms and legs faster, weaving in and out of tree trunks. She found one of her rare, genuine smiles spreading across her dirt-streaked face. She was still a little ways behind the pack but she didn't care. For the first time since she was left alone in this cursed loop forest, she felt alive. She felt free, unbothered by the ground digging into her bare feet as they impacted.

Unable to contain herself, she let out a loud whoop of something that resembled joy. The Voice didn't try to speak to her for the rest of the night. Perhaps It knew Its words would be falling on deaf ears.

She didn't catch anything herself during the hunt, but she was able to see the variety of survival spots where the wolves sourced their game. One was another clearing, about half the size of the wolves' current place of residence. A single tree stood proud in the center of the space. A different one was a peculiar patch of forest permeated with draping vines, which Kaitlyn recognized as jasmine, albeit the telling white flowers were only just beginning to bud. She thought it was curiously pretty, although it was a little ominous at night. There were other spots, too. Each one just as unique in their appearance.

Before they all returned to the cave, Kaitlyn took a detour to her original clearing to collect the tent and her sleeping bag. It was a bitter homecoming, going back to where it all began. She was glad to be leaving the memories staining the scenery behind.

By the time she finally lugged everything back into the cave, huffing and puffing, the sun was beginning to peek above the horizon, casting the lower part of the sky into a flared ombre of pink and orange. Amazing to her that even at rock bottom, beauty still found a way to reach its depths.

She gazed in awe for a few moments, enjoying the pleasantly cool gusts of wind that carried with them the scents of the earth. As she watched, she heard the distinct phrase 'the sky is always bigger than our problems' meander through her brain. She reckoned the phrase came from her mom, seeing as her dad was more the practical type and Lilly was too busy worrying over boys and makeup to have much insight into anything, but she wasn't certain. It didn't make much sense to her, seeing as problems weren't physical things, but she found comfort in it anyway. A few moments later and she was back to work, finding her daily rabbit near the mouth of the cave. As she padded through the entrance to retrieve her knife, she caught a glimpse of the other wolves savagely tearing into two deer. She strolled out of the cave with a shrug, not sparing the sight a second glance. She went about preparing her meal the way she always did.

Adrenaline continued to buzz beneath her skin. Feeling restless, she went to the edge of the lake.

Due to the calm clarity of the water, Kaitlyn was able to see her reflection rather well. She lowered her head closer to the surface, baring her teeth. Humming, she tried to recall the last time she'd cleaned them. Had it been a week? Two? "Too long" was the resounding answer.

She made a beeline for the trees, launching herself into the air and snagging the tip of a branch.

Back on solid ground, she was instantly battered with the memory of a peculiar moment she'd experienced many fortnights ago.

Day 17 into her abandonment, she facepalmed after waking up with creaky teeth and sore gums.

Of course, she had to brush her teeth. She had no idea why the thought hadn't crossed her mind until then. Upon taking a moment to wonder how she was meant to brush her teeth; another memory began to take shape in her mind.

Last year in fourth grade, her class had been required to check out a book from the library for an independent research project. If she remembered correctly the title of the one she'd chosen had been 'Living Off the Land: A Beginners Guide to Survival.' It had been a little advanced for her age, and she'd had to have her dad read and explain the big words to her, but she stuck with it.

One of the topics it covered was methods to clean one's teeth when not in possession of traditional materials. The text described using a twig from a dogwood, oak or maple tree as a makeshift toothbrush. To do so, one needed to bite one end of the stick until it splintered into strips resembling bristles, then simply use it accordingly.

She had done just that, using a twig from one of the surrounding oak trees.

"Figures," The Voice had uttered.

"Whoht?!" she'd barked, her voice slightly distorted from the twig still stuck in her mouth.

"Just my **fortune that I end up with a child with some** semblance of a brain and how to use it," The Voice had continued, seemingly unaware Kaitlyn had spoken.

When she had heard nothing more after a few moments, she'd rolled her eyes and resumed her brushing.

Kaitlyn was snapped back to the present when a large brown leaf surfing on the wind currents attacked her face. She exclaimed in surprise and promptly used her twig to karate chop the offending object from the air.

She stomped it into the dirt for good measure.

After giving the crushed leaf a dirty look, she directed her attention back to her twig, determining the length was sufficient. She gazed back into the forest only for her eyes to light up when she noticed the most diminutive of green beginning to sprout from the boughs of the trees. She did a giddy little jig, realizing spring must be coming.

Skipping back to the lake with her twig in hand, she dropped to her knees, gnawed on the wood for a few moments, stuck the split ends into the water and went to town on her mouth. It tasted strange, an odd mixture of dirt and something intensely bitter, but she found she didn't mind it after a while. She couldn't help but long for a normal toothbrush or the overbearing taste of mint. And new clothes. She looked down at herself, still brushing away. Her mom would definitely call it risqué, considering anything from the waist down was essentially scraps of soiled fabric held together by flimsy bits of thread. It was no longer a lavender color; dingier gray now with various stains of who knew what.

Making a disgusted face, she surmised that she'd have to do something about that.

Once she finished brushing her teeth, she threw the stick as far as she could into the lake; It landed with a little plop some yards out. She scooped up some of the water and splashed it in her face, scrubbing lightly to get rid of the smudges. Goosebumps erupted along her skin. The weather may have been approaching warmer spring temperatures, but the water certainly hadn't received the memo yet.

After washing, she debated going over to the waterfall for a drink. When she found her mouth stretching into a wide yawn, she shrugged and found she couldn't be bothered.

Instead, she shuffled back into the cave, stifling a second yawn with her hand, suddenly overcome with a wave of weariness. She dragged her sleeping bag she had retrieved from the tent earlier and placed it near the other wolves.

Slipping inside, she shifted around until she found a comfortable position. She really missed her own bed. She missed hot baths and clean clothes and an actual hairbrush. She found she missed a lot of material things, not just her family.

She felt tears begin to blur her vision but didn't dare let them fall. It was times like this, when she just wouldn't cry or scream to let everything out, where she felt like she was drowning, sinking deeper into an ocean of isolation. One that had no intention of allowing her another breath at the surface.

She'd get out of this forest.

She'd see her family again.

She squeezed her eyes shut and forced the exhaustion to take over, to allow the tender caress of sleep to make everything go away for a while. She was out in minutes, the tension leaving her shoulders.

Maybe one day she'd finally be able to breathe normal again.

<div align="center">~~~~~~~~~~</div>

It was nearing the end of April, verging on May, when Kaitlyn finally managed to catch her first doe. She'd successfully caught rabbits before, but they weren't big enough for what she had in mind. Catching the dang thing was no easy feat, and more than a little embarrassing. All that could be said was...she just...went for it.

When the deer was finally slain, Kaitlyn still panting from the exertion, The Voice, who had decided to renew their relationship, simply remarked, *"That was ridiculous."*

With a profound scowl twisting her lips, Kaitlyn promptly snapped, *"Shut up!"* and proceeded to follow the wolves back to the cave, or what she'd begun to call camp. All the while thinking that she had a lot to learn, but she wasn't about to let The Voice become privy to that particular notion.

That was the beginning of her 'shut up' phase. The Voice once informed her, rather snarky, that it was akin to listening to a broken record, which Kaitlyn responded with yet another 'shut up.'

After she had returned to camp and thanked the deer for its sacrifice, something her dad had once informed her was a sign of respect, she'd skinned the animal very carefully so that the resulting skin remained intact. She proceeded to eat her fill of the meat and scrub the pelt clean in the shimmering lake, making sure to scrape away any remaining fat and flesh like she'd seen her dad do. She had already fashioned a new pair of underwear from the material of the tent, so now all she had to do was replace her nightgown with something less mangled. What little of her nightgown still existed, looked as if she'd been mauled by a bear.

Once she finished washing the skin, she laid it out on a flat rock to dry. After a week filled with periodic manipulation and stretching of the damp fur, she moved on to tanning.

She cracked open the deer's skull using a rock, her face locked into a grimace. She removed the brain matter and mashed it into the pelt, on the verge of gagging the entire time. She'd learned about this method from a school field trip to a nearby indigenous reservation, thankfully remembering how they had explained early tribe practices. She left it sit for a few more days. The next step was to continue stretching and bending the skin until it became pliable, and all the brain matter was rubbed off. Finally, she hung the pelt over the fire for a few hours, letting the smoke seep into the skin, with a little help from her flapping hands.

When the process was complete, she took the skin and wrapped it around herself to gage how much of it she would need. When that was taken care of, she spread the fur out horizontally. It was somewhat shaped like a stout rectangle, with each of the corners extended because of the legs.

After staring at the thing like it was going to magically transform into an article of clothing by itself, she eventually crouched down and used her knife to painstakingly cut the short ends of the rectangle into strips until they were long enough to be knotted together. She knew she could use the bone and sinew from the animal to sew the fabric together, but she lacked the practical knowledge to make that happen.

Next, she grasped the first strip on each end, brought them together and double knotted them where the slit in the fur ended. She experimented with different ways of tying with the rest of the strips to have as few gaps within the dress as possible. She eventually settled on an intricate design that resembled a french braid. The remaining fur at the end was double knotted and trimmed to neat little stubs, but still long enough to ensure nothing came undone.

When the finished product was clutched to her chest, she scoured the clearing for a secluded place to change. Her eyes landed on the cave, except the wolves were in there and though animals they may have been, she was not going to change in front of them, comprehension of nudity or not. A familiar shiver of discomfort creeped over her as she remembered her dog Teddy would force his way into the bathroom when she was about to shower and stare at her as she undressed. Her mom would always tell her it was a nosy thing dogs did and that they didn't understand, but it never made her feel any less self-conscious.

Her gaze eventually slid over to the waterfall.

Surely there had to be some sort of nook she could temporarily hunker in so she could dress. She'd never taken much time to sniff around there before, let alone bother going over at all unless it was to quench her thirst.

Trotting over, she began her search.

She didn't have to search for long, because sure enough, right as she rounded the rock, the cave disappearing from view, there was a small, seemingly naturally occurring alcove molded into the stone. She pursed her lips at it; It felt too easy. It looked suspiciously like a door, albeit concave, which didn't help ease her mistrust of it. She slipped inside anyway.

The top of her head and her shoulders grazed the craggy walls and ceiling of the nook. She stepped into her fur 'dress' except for the very top hole before yanking it up until the material of her nightgown was bunched at her waist and draping over the deer skin. She slipped her arms out of her nightgown and proceeded to tug the fuzzy dress until it was under her armpits. She wasted no time ripping the nightgown over her head, dropping it at her feet. Finally, she took the strap she hadn't stepped into and jerked it over her head where the knot settled at the base of her neck, resembling a haphazard halter top.

She signed contentedly at finally wearing something clean, feeling a surge of pride in her chest. She smiled, tenderly running her hands along the high neckline at her collarbone and fingers brushing the hemline that fell generously to the tops of her knees.

She was about to take a step, completely oblivious to the literal *rags* pooling around her, when her feet became tangled. As she attempted to free one foot, she jerked too hard and caused the material to slip out from beneath her other foot. Thus, leading her to stagger backwards, nails scraping uselessly on the gray-brown walls of the 'alcove' as she tried to catch herself.

It wasn't that big of a deal, there should've been a wall about a foot behind her, so she didn't have to fall far. She *should've* stopped falling. Her back *should've* collided with solid rock. That wasn't what happened.

She passed through the rock as if there was nothing but empty space behind her. It was only when she awkwardly landed on her side with an abrupt wince that she found her voice with a shrill 'whope!' escaping her lips. Her eyes had slammed shut right before impact, so she dubiously peeked one open, moderately surprised she was still in one piece.

She eventually opened both eyes, a question edging on her tongue. Though it died as she did a double take when she saw a wall of bumpy, slick gray stone in front of her.

She was hit with the deafening roar of rushing water that wasn't that loud five seconds ago. She whipped her head around and was met with yet another wall, this one made of a clear veil of cascading water.

She scrambled to her feet and stared at it, taking a few teetering steps forward as if in a trance, realizing that she could decipher indistinct shapes and blurred colors through the water. She first noticed the large black blob slightly off center that fell in a stark contrast to the sea of smeared green and brown in the background.

'Wait a second....am I–?'

Her head whisked back and forth so fast it was a wonder she didn't make herself dizzy. She was in some sort of small cavern, the walls glossy with water leaking from the ceiling.

"...Huh. Guess I'm behind the waterfall...." she breathed in awe. *'But wait.'*

Her fascination fading, she glared at the back wall as if it had physically assaulted her. To be fair, it kind of had.

"I knew it!" she declared to no one in particular, her hand shooting out to point accusingly at the wall.

'I knew there was something suspicious about that door shaped hollow! Nothing's ever been that convenient in this forest!'

Despite her offense, she had to admit, this place was kind of cool. As she continued to observe, she noticed that there was moss speckling various places on the wall and floor, making the cavern appear as if it was afflicted by green and brown warts, lichens hanging from the ceiling like hair.

She glanced around the small cave with mirth dancing in her eyes. "It's a witch cave. It made me think that it was a normal wall and then it lured me in here like a witch would," she reasoned out loud.

'But how do I get out?'

She eyed the waterfall, then eyed her new dress. She shook her head. No way.

That meant her only other option was to go back out the way she came in. She raised an eyebrow at the back wall and proceeded to take halting steps forward as if she expected it to bite her. For all she knew, it might. All bets were off at this point. When she reached the wall, she tentatively began to feel along it.

She reached the area where she thought she must have fallen through before and was–

'Dang it not again!'

She managed to put her arms out to catch herself this time but that did little to keep the dust from the ground out of her mouth. Practically seething, she pushed herself to her feet, whirled around, reared her head back, and spat at the place she recently came from. It was a gesture her mom would deem unlady-like, but she was far past the point of caring because she still had *dirt in her mouth.*

She caught sight of her pile of rags on the ground that had instigated this whole fiasco and scowled at it.

"This is your fault," she hissed, her eyes narrowing as she proceeded to kick the offending fabric until it disappeared into the undergrowth.

With a huff and a firm nod, she spun on her heel and marched back to the cave with the early afternoon sun casting her in golden light.

CHAPTER SEVEN
All These Children, That Have Been Saved

She wasn't prepared the first time it happened.

There she was, staring down the first human faces she'd seen in months as the shrill whistle pierced the air, prying itself into the minds of the two adults who stood rigid in front of her.

~~~~~~~~~

Kaitlyn had left with the wolves that night expecting a normal hunt. She'd failed to realize they were leading her back to the beginning until it was right on top of her. She was passing through the treeline before she could stop her momentum.

Feet transcending from dirt to grass, she'd frozen on the spot, her eyes resembling a deer caught in headlights, her mouth falling ajar as she took in the scene before her: the large orange tent and the two adults swaying on their feet a few yards from the tent, as if they were moving to a melody only they could hear.

Upon the initial incredulity, her next sentiment was relief. Maybe these people could help her escape. She almost threw caution to the wind and bolted over to them, her toes curling in the grass in preparation, but she'd caught sight of the forest around her: still looped. So long as the forest remained in that state, she wasn't going anywhere. Her heart deflated.

She was vaguely aware of the wolves slowly skulking out of the clearing, but before she could fully comprehend the
~~~~~~~~~

sight, a rustle drew her attention back in front of her.

Without a conscious thought, she crept forward on damp earth with feet that had learned the art of silence. As she passed in front of the tent, she had the sudden urge to look at it, and when she did, she scarcely managed to suppress a gasp. The flap of the tent was partially unzipped, and nestled snugly in a single red sleeping bag was a little boy that couldn't have been more than ten years old. With the scant moonlight filtering through the trees, casting the inside of the space in a shadowy orange hue, she was able to see he had wild golden hair that spread across his pillow like a halo.

She shifted her focus over to the male and female that must have been the boy's parents, who were shuffling in a sporadic manner, their heels attempting to dig into the earth as if in protest of their motion.

Kaitlyn narrowed her eyes, *'Wait a minute.'*

The realization of what she was witnessing hit her with the blunt force of an oncoming train. She staggered forward a few steps before regaining her composure and sprinting over to the adults. She stopped directly in front of them, blocking their path. Their shuffling ceased, leaving them rigid pillars before her. They were weighed down with their belongings, well, sans the few pieces of equipment they'd left behind. If she needed any further convincing about what was going on, she got it.

Words like 'stupid' and 'foolish' were bouncing around her mind, but she could reprimand herself later.

Right now, she had to–

Then she heard it again.

That all too familiar whistle.

The man and woman moved to bypass her, but she blocked their way again, her hands outstretched in a gesture that screamed 'stop.'

The whistle increased in volume.

"Don't listen to it," she whispered strickenly, eyes boring desperate holes into their expressionless faces.

She attempted to catch the blue eyes of the woman, but they stared right through her like Kaitlyn wasn't there at all. The same was true for the man; no one seemed to be home inside, their faces appearing to be crafted from stone. Kaitlyn wondered if it was already too late.

Dread dragged its spindly fingers up her spine. She gritted her teeth.

Steeling herself, she blurted the first thing that came to her mind: "Wake up!"

The couple blinked.

"You can't leave your son here! So just wake up!" she shouted, her desperation rising.

They tried to evade her.

She once again moved in front of them. "Stop! Cover your ears, don't listen!" She turned her head toward the tree line as the whistle continued. "I know you're doing this, you stupid Voice! Knock it off and let them go!"

The whistle intensified.

"Please just leave them alone!" she pleaded.

Yet again, the parents tried to side-step around her.

She moved to hinder them, tears beginning to burn in her eyes. "Wake up! You don't know what you're doing! Don't listen to It! You're making a bad choice, you can't abandon him!"

She startled when she heard rustling from the direction of the tent, hastily sticking her head around the adults at the same moment the little boy from before emerged from the tent, one hand rubbing lazily at the side of his face.

Kaitlyn's eyes nearly popped out of her head.

Once the sleepiness began to recede, the boy dropping his hand, he regarded the current scene with a look of dopey confusion.

"Mom? Dad? Where're you going?" he slurred drowsily.

The whistle abruptly ceased.

At the sound of their son's voice, the parents flinched

simultaneously and appeared to come back to themselves. They blinked dazedly, perplexed looks on both their faces, as if they had no idea where they were.

Kaitlyn was glad her auto pilot took over and forced her to dart into the treeline. She hid behind a thick tree, plastering her back to the trunk. She placed a palm to her chest. It felt as if her heart was trying to thunder right through her skin. Still attempting to catch her breath, she peeked out from behind the tree and nearly sighed with relief as she saw the parents deconstructing the tent.

When they finished packing the rest of their gear, the mom made a grab for her bewildered son, who had been standing nearby.

Before they started moving, however, the boy, still groggy, asked, "Mom, who was that girl?"

Kaitlyn's previously thundering heartbeat suddenly froze, the organ suspended in a free-fall in her chest.

Why she didn't want them to know she was there was beyond her. She couldn't leave anyway, so what was the point? As much as she despised the fact, it *was* the bitter truth at the moment.

The parents furrowed their brows.

"Girl? What girl, sweetie?" the mom asked gently.

Katlyn sagged against the tree trunk.

Slightly exasperated, the boy elaborated, "The girl with the messy hair that was just standing in front of you over there."

He pointed to the spot Kaitlyn had previously occupied.

She waited with bated breath.

The dad's thick brows furrowed further. "Josh, what are you talking about? We weren't over there and there was no girl. You must have been seeing things, the night does that sometimes."

Kaitlyn held back a snort at the last part.

Apparently, the boy's name was Josh.

Well, Josh looked like he was about to argue, but his dad

silenced him with a stern look.

Not giving up so easily, Josh fired off another question. "Then why are we leaving? We just got here."

The mom gave the impression of being moderately uncomfortable as she warily glanced around the moonlit clearing. Her form was stiff as she pulled her son closer to her.

The dad narrowed his eyes, scanning the shadowy depths of the surrounding forest.

Kaitlyn managed to jerk back behind the tree before he saw her.

"Somethin' ain't right, and I refuse to let us stick around to find out what," he said.

'That's a massive understatement' Kaitlyn thought sarcastically. *'Look at you, playing it cool,'* she stifled a derisive scoff. If he knew what actually went bump in the night around here, he would've left everything behind, tent and all, and had his family halfway home already.

Though she quickly sobered when she saw the family hurrying from the clearing, the son eagerly peering into the forest as if expecting the girl to appear again.

Kaitlyn was about to follow them as a last-ditch attempt to leave the forest, but as soon as they passed beyond the trees, that plan flew right out the proverbial window as the family literally disappeared before her eyes.

She didn't even have time to be surprised before she was verbally assaulted.

"You insolent little BRAT!" The Voice roared.

Kaitlyn flinched.

Unsuitably frigid gusts of wind instantly came out of nowhere, clawing at her hair and clothes, howling chillingly through the loop forest. The whispers commenced, harshly caressing her ears as the shadows came alive, thrashing and writhing with scarcely contained violence.

Her body stiffened, her blood running cold, her eyes

bulging, her heart battering against her rib cage and pounding so loud in her ears it nearly drowned out the wind. Sweat trickled down the back of her neck and the side of her face. Why couldn't she move?

"Do you understand what you have done!?"

The shadows surged toward her at a startling speed, but she was still stuck, dread racing through her veins as the wall of blackness closed in on her.

A sharp bark pierced the air, sounding like deliverance, and the shadows momentarily recoiled.

Kaitlyn seized the opportunity and ran. She was running so fast she couldn't feel the forest floor beneath her feet. Branches clawed at her face and arms. She felt something warm and wet drip down her cheek. She couldn't feel the pain; the shadows were hot on her trail, thrashing at her ankles.

Suddenly the wolves were around her, flanking both her sides and her back as she took the lead. She could no longer feel the press of the shadows at her back, but she didn't dare let herself believe that meant she was safe.

A sound unlike anything she had ever heard burst from the surrounding darkness. A guttural, demonic roar that could have only come from the most wicked of places. It was the savage of all things. Her steps momentarily faltered as it dug its claws into her core. It reverberated through the air, filling up the space to the brim with its revolting sound. It was hunger and rage personified, something so vile that it could have easily split the earth right down to its center. Somewhere out in the universe, two galaxies collided, meeting their calamitous end.

She regained her footing when the wolves insistently nosed her forward, but the roar, no, the *moan*-that utterly sickening, viscid sound that no being should ever have to hear-didn't stop. But God, she wished it would. Or that she could tear her ears off, or *something,* just to make it stop.

After mere minutes, which felt like hours, she finally saw the camp through the trees and almost cried with relief.

As she was about to break the treeline, The Voice snarled, *"This is **not** over!"*

With that promise freezing her rushing blood, she took the last step into the camp...and promptly threw up.

Once her stomach stopped trying to become the impossible knot, she unbent herself, dragging the back of her trembling hand across her soiled mouth.

'Ugh, gross,' she internally groaned.

Still shaking, she attempted to kick dirt over the mess before hastily staggering away from the damp splotch on the ground. She only managed a few feet before crumpling in a heap, her face buried in her hands and shoulders quaking.

Midnight began to trot forward, but paused as Kaitlyn made a noise.

The wolf cocked her head to the side when the sound came a second time.

Then laughter filled the air.

Loud, hysterical cackling that burst forth from her as she threw her head back.

The laughing continued with multiple attempts to stifle it only for it to come roaring back, sounding more deranged each time it did.

She couldn't fathom what was wrong with her. This couldn't be normal. What just happened was as far from funny as one could get. You didn't just *laugh* after nearly having the life ripped from your bones.

She somehow ended up on her side clutching her abdomen, tears mixing with the blood running down her face. She couldn't stop, even as it stole her breath until she was wheezing, it kept forcing itself out, her mind unable to string together a coherent thought.

Midnight and the other wolves, having formed a semicircle around the trembling human mass, remained as still as statues, showing no signs of moving until her wheezing subsided.

She was eventually reduced to hiccup giggles before they faded away into simple labored breathing and finally ceasing altogether.

When she was able to think clearly again, she sat up, wondering why she'd reacted like that. She had likely just escaped a rather ugly death and she freaking *laughed* about it. Who did that? Her heart was still racing from the near miss, but with her mind no longer clouded, she realized she'd never felt more alive. The flood of adrenaline just mere minutes before had eased into a pleasant buzz coursing through her body. She'd even prevented that boy from suffering her same fate, which brought a blinding smile to her blood-streaked face.

Granted, The Voice's enraged, vindictive parting words left a sinking feeling in her gut, but she knew she'd put herself in the same position all over again if it meant she could spare another life. Plus, she finally had something over The Voice, a thought that nearly caused a relapse in her cackling.

Kaitlyn: 1.

Scratchy Voice: 0.
She did take the time, however, to mull over her actions, briefly entertaining the thought that she might have been one of those adrenaline junkies her sister had mentioned in a conversation before. That would've explained her abnormal reaction. Or maybe it was a defense mechanism. Either way, she kept herself from thinking too hard about it, and before the thought of her sister could leave a pang in her chest, she turned her attention to the variation of canine eyes boring into her.

Kaitlyn, now slightly self-conscious over the episode they had just witnessed in her, instinctively crossed her arms over her chest, snapping, "What?!"

That seemed to break the tension because Midnight was suddenly bounding up to her. Without warning, the wolf lapped a big, wet kiss up the entire length of Kaitlyn's face.

She immediately recoiled, her face scrunching up as she vigorously scrubbed at her now slick skin.

"Midniiiiight, why'd you do that?!" she whined shrilly, proceeding to look down at the slobber and blood on her palm with a curled lip, "Ugh, it's so gross!" she exclaimed, throwing the culprit a dirty look.

The only response Kaitlyn received was an eagerly wagging tail.

She rolled her eyes.

Midnight yawned.

"Okay, now you're just mocking me."

The black wolf made a noise that suspiciously resembled a snort.

Rolling her eyes again, Kaitlyn lugged herself to her feet and pointedly turned her back on Midnight, her shoulders sagging and the lines on her face softening at the turn of the atmosphere. She shuffled over to the lake, dropping down to her knees once she reached the water's edge.

The soft sound of pawsteps followed by a muffled thump behind her alerted her she'd been followed.

She paid it no mind as she leaned forward to gaze at her watery reflection. Her eyes widened slightly as she made out what appeared to be numerous cuts and slick ribbons of blood littering her face.

That was when the sting of the wounds hit her. She had a few minor nicks along her jaw and some more concerning scratches across each of her cheeks, but the one she really had to worry about was the deep gash at her right temple, which was leaking a steady flow of deep crimson down the length of her face.

While Kaitlyn knew most head wounds appeared worse than what they were, she still intended to keep an eye on it. The last thing she needed–or wanted–was an infection.

She began splashing water in her face to wash off the blood and remaining wolf slaver, hissing when the water intensified the sting. She intended to smack around some of the offending branches the next time she got the chance. Petty? Most likely. Did she care? Definitely not.

When she finished, she firmly pressed the heel of her palm against her temple, steadily adding pressure to try and staunch the bleeding. She rose to her feet and padded back to the cave, Midnight on her heels. Once at the entrance she stuck her hand in the nook in the cave wall and pulled out one of the cleaned patches of animal fur she'd stored there just in case she found a use for it.

As she replaced her hand with the soft fur, she noticed the wolves had settled down at the cave's rear while she'd been cleaning her cuts. Dawn wasn't far off.

Making her way further into the space, she set a mental reminder for herself to look for some coneflowers when she next woke up. According to one of the books she'd once read, if consumed, they were supposed to help prevent infection.

Kaitlyn heaved a heavy sigh that bore the burden of too many shackles. It was the weight of a person who'd endured a brutally long, hard, and taxing life, not that of an 11 year old girl.

She was practically dead on her feet, the terror that had sent the rush through her not even an hour ago finally taking its toll.

The events of that night only proved to solidify the fact that even if she was strong and capable enough to escape the forest, it wouldn't be for a very long time. Considering how Josh and his parents vanished when they'd crossed into the trees, she managed to scrape together that the forest wasn't looped for them. Consequently, they were able to leave uninhibited and they disappeared because Kaitlyn couldn't see the real unlooped forest. So even if she had made them aware of her presence and tried to leave with them, it would have been pointless because they were each seeing something entirely different.

If she were being honest, it felt like a reality slap in the face. Though the action didn't exactly have the desired effect.

She'd already come to a melancholic acceptance even if she hadn't been aware of it until that moment. Her hope, drive and fiery determination remained steady, but she now understood getting out wouldn't be as easy as she originally thought.

Physically unable to remain upright any longer, she collapsed into a heap, uncaring of being on hard ground instead of her sleeping bag. She situated herself on her right side to keep the fur firmly pressed to her gash while she slept and was swept away by unconsciousness in the amount of time it took to snap a finger.

~~~~~~~~~~

She awoke mid-day to a fierce, throbbing ache on the back of her ankles. When she became marginally coherent, she groggily lifted her head and glanced down to see angry red welts, along with some scratches adorning both her achilles.

She sighed heavily, carelessly letting her head thwack onto the ground, ignoring the burst of pain that followed. She buried her face into her arms and willed herself back into sleep's comforting embrace, wanting to forget for just a little while longer.

~~~~~~~~~~

A little over three weeks later, it happened again. Prior to, Kaitlyn had purposefully avoided the forest beyond the camp after the first incident to allow The Voice time to cool down and take Its equivalent of a chill pill. When she did venture back out, the rage had simmered down to bitterness, deeming it safe for her to continue hunting. While The Voice never tried anything with the shadows during that time, Its verbal abuse became flat out obnoxious. Sometimes It would start randomly grumbling moodily like a child that was told 'no.' Oftentimes, Kaitlyn had to prevent herself from laughing in The Voice's non-existent face on more than one occasion.

The second occurrence was similar to the first, the main difference being that instead of a single boy, it was two twin girls around the same age as that Josh kid.

While she verbally still tried to wake the parents and stand in the way to prevent their departure, she simultaneously threw pieces of whatever was on the ground at the tent until the dark-haired girls awoke. When they emerged from the tent, wondering aloud what was going on, the parents snapped out of their trance and Kaitlyn bolted from view. The wolves immediately encircled her as the shadows shifted and twitched restlessly, seemingly agitated. For a reason Kaitlyn had yet to fathom, The Blackness couldn't hurt the wolves, and as long as the creatures stood between her and the night around her, then It couldn't hurt her either.

Just as before, the family packed up their belongings while the kids wondered about who the 'mysterious' girl was, following up with the parents having no idea what their children were talking about. Both adults produced some excuse about seeing things and were quick to pull a vanishing act as they passed the treeline.

The Voice's anger was not nearly as monstrous as last time, but rather a quiet and seething, yet petulant fury that had the shadows churning aggressively, steam rolling off them in stifling waves. The Voice, however, did not make a sound.

At least, not until Kaitlyn started giggling with maniacal glee as she trotted with the wolves back to camp.

The Voice released an animalistic snarling sound; Kaitlyn only cackled harder, seemingly unbothered that the shadows began to hiss nor that she was practically dancing on the precipice of her own grave.

The wind intensified, howling at Kaitlyn, the branches above thrashing ferociously. Leaves and bits of twig rained down on her and the wolves. She skidded to a halt as a thought hit her, her vibrant eyes wide.

"...*No way~,*" she snickered to herself as the wolves came to a halt beside her.

"*What!?*" The Scratchy Voice bit out.

Kaitlyn clamped her lips closed to keep from laughing again, settling on an impish grin instead. "Scratchy Voice, are you throwing a temper tantrum?" she inquired slowly with a teasing lilt.

The wind died instantly. The movement of the tree branches came to a standstill and the churning shadows sunk back into ordinary darkness.

It was clear The Voice didn't deem any further response necessary.

When Kaitlyn realized as such, she continued on her merry way, and if there was a smug little smile on her face, well, there was no one around to see it anyway.

~~~~~~~~~

It was nearing the end of summer the third time it happened. Though this time, accompanying the parents and a young girl was another female who appeared to be around her mid to late teens.

'Like Lilly...' Kaitlyn thought vacantly.

She swatted the realization away at once and returned to hurling sticks and pebbles at the tent to wake the younger girl inside.

When the girl finally poked her head out, eyes squinted and rasping out an annoyed 'What?', the parents and the
~~~~~~~~~

older teen, who was most likely the sister, grimaced and snapped out of their zombie-like state.

The high-pitched whistle cut off.

Like usual.

Kaitlyn darted into the trees out of sight.

Like usual.

The wolves swarmed her in their protective circle.

That was expected.

What deviated from the past two instances was the pang of...*something*, that shot fiercely through her chest and left a bitter taste in her mouth, causing her to slightly stagger at the sheer intensity of it. It settled at the center of her sternum as she watched the family prepare for departure.

The scene sent a rather unpleasant and unwanted wave of nostalgia washing over her. The way the young girl and her supposed older sister interacted reminded Kaitlyn too much of what she once had. What was currently beyond her reach.

That *something* from earlier reared its ugly head, strengthening the ache in the center of her chest to the point where Kaitlyn had the fleeting thought that it might consume her.

But she knew what it was. It wasn't a feeling she was overly familiar with, something she'd felt only sparingly during her life. Nothing like this, though.

Acknowledging it only seemed to give it more power, spreading through her blood stream like a disease. It seeped into her bones, wrapped around the tendons and sinew, lodged itself in the dark corners and started to make a home.

She found herself entertaining the thought of what might have transpired had she not intercepted the parent's and sister's retreat, if she had allowed the little girl to be left alone at the mercy of The Voice. This dark and twisted part of her wanted the other girl to know how it felt to have her family snatched away from her, to endure the trauma Kaitlyn had to deal with. That part wished she hadn't halted the family's abandonment, at least then she would no longer have to suffer alone. Misery loved company, after all.

She had been robbed of what was right in front of her. Each receding back mocked her, rubbed salt in the still gaping wound, reminding her of what she no longer had. No one was around to help when *she* needed it. No one was there to stop *her* parents and sister from leaving, so why should she save others from desertion when no one saved her? She was glaring at the family with a look filled with so much hatred it could have been a tangible force.

'It's not fair! Why does she get to go home and be with her family while I'm still stuck out here, unable to leave this awful place!?

Her hands shook with poorly concealed rage and jealousy. The shadows around her trembled in giddy anticipation.

A wolf suddenly pressed his nose into her palm and just like that, she was collapsing to her knees, all anger and hate and envy dissipating. Unshed tears obscured her vision as she watched the family disappear from the clearing.

'It's not their fault....' Kaitlyn thought, although a little begrudgingly.

She knew that.

She also knew her previous thoughts were selfish, that they weren't really what she felt, merely what the irrational and callous part of her brain latched onto. She would've been ashamed if there was actually someone around to witness her transgression.

Only, there wasn't.

Not anymore.

She protested the appearance of her tears, furiously scrubbing at her eyes and attempting to suppress the ache in her chest. She didn't want that girl to endure the same fate. She didn't want to feel like she was always drowning. She didn't want to cry anymore. She just wanted to go *home.*

'*One day,*' a voice in her head supplied gently, a breath present one moment and gone the next, vanishing like a ghost done haunting.

The salty wetness gradually dried from Kaitlyn's eyes, the ache becoming less prominent. She stood up.

Things wouldn't get better for a long time. Neither would the pain. Her family didn't remember her, but she clung to the hope that she could and would make them remember anyway. Until she found a way to escape the loop forest, she'd just have to keep pushing herself through another day, enjoy the little things that lessened the burden on her shoulders and made her feel alive, if only for a few moments at a time. She'd have her bad days, days where all hope seemed lost and that she'd never see her family again. Those days were inevitable. She'd already had her fair share and it hadn't even been a year, but she always came out on the other side, sometimes a little more worse for wear than before, but still kicking. The wolves were there to support her when she fell, and The Scratchy Voice had become more of a nuisance than anything else. She vowed to see the world beyond the forest again, even if it was the last thing she ever did.

She had to. There was no other option.

An enigmatic expression washed over her face as she gazed into the moon dappled clearing. It wasn't quite a smile that held her mouth, but it wasn't a frown either.

Perhaps a minute, wry quirk of the lips.

"Yeah. One day."

CHAPTER EIGHT
THE END OF DARKNESS

The following winter passed in a misty haze. Kaitlyn evaded the symptoms of frostbite and experienced minimal mishaps with The Voice. In fact, more often than not, she forgot It existed at all.

When The Voice did venture to speak, It sounded weary, having lost Its usual snarkiness. The shadows seemed to move more sluggishly too. It was almost too good to be true.

How morbid was it of her that she almost missed their conversations? Even if all they consisted of were insults and manipulation.

Just how lonely did a person have to be to yearn for interaction from an evil entity that tried to kill them?

Maybe she was going crazy.

When the silence grew too insufferable, she broke out into random, spontaneous monologues about the most mundane things just to keep herself talking. One time, she went on and on about how stupid winter was with its stupid rain, and its stupid snow, and its stupid cold temperatures. In another instance she had a screaming match with a thunderstorm. 'You think you're so tough because you're all big and intimidating and can make scary noises, but guess what sky, I can make scary noises too! Raawwwrrrgggg!'

Her eyes often lightened with amusement at that particular memory.

And yet, she still found herself fighting the consuming impulse to let herself go again and withdraw into the depths of her mind. She did her best to distract herself, to leave the past where it belonged and instead focus on the expansive feeling she had that her chance at a homecoming with her family was drawing closer.

There was also a sinking feeling too, one she constantly pushed back against, refusing to consider what it could possibly mean.

The forest remained looped, but there were minor changes over time, hinting something was amiss. Where before she witnessed no signs of birds, now they were everywhere, rudely waking her with their absurdly shrill chirping at the crest of dawn. Bugs also began to appear, much to her distaste. Little iridescent, multi-colored beetles and ants each place she went.

Whatever was happening, she prayed it was linked to The Voice's progressively weakening state.

When winter progressed into spring, The Voice seemed to perk up slightly, reacquiring a little of Its familiar sarcasm and insistence regarding the circumstances surrounding her abandonment. The jabs were more for show now. For old times' sake.

The Voice's attitude steadily improved with the rising temperatures, eventually returning to Its previous spirit. Though as summer wore on and without a breath of other human life to be seen, The Voice's mood gradually decreased again. Until one mid-August night.

The shadows were more violent than ever, lashing out wildly and hissing at Kaitlyn and her pack. They smothered everything beyond the treeline and heavily obstructed the moon. If it weren't for the wolves creating a bubble around her, she would have been drowning in an ocean of inky blackness.

It was two boys she saved that night, friends most likely, considering they looked nothing alike and there were two sets of adults. When she darted back into the forest among the wolves, The Voice immediately began snarling and cursing at her, attempting to fling shadows at her to no avail. She hardly spared a glance to the thrashing tendrils.

Its voice still sounded weak, so It didn't have the desired effect that It once did. She instead settled for watching the two families gather their belongings.

As she regarded their retreating forms, the two boys insisting they saw someone as they were ushered along, she felt an overwhelming urge to *move*, and suddenly her legs were striding forward without her permission. Her eyes grew comically wide with alarm, a small, strangled noise of protest leaving her mouth. It was like a string was attached to her and someone was pulling it, because no matter what she screamed in her head, her body wouldn't listen to her. She stopped as soon as she was beyond the trees, her panic inexplicably vanishing as she stood there calmly in plain sight should any of the individuals in front of her turn around.

One of the kids glanced over his shoulder, a boy around Kaitlyn's age with dark messy hair and as many freckles as there were stars in the sky. The other boy followed suit, also around Kaitlyn's age and sporting flaming red locks. Both of their eyes widened as they froze mid-step, lips parting on a syllable neither of them were capable of finishing.

Kaitlyn didn't know what kind of look was on her face or how she must have appeared in their eyes. Wild and dirty perhaps. The two boys rubbed their eyes simultaneously, possibly to ensure she wasn't a figment of their sleep-disoriented minds; Kaitlyn took advantage of the moment to slink silently back into the trees, watching as the boys were yanked from their perplexed stupor and dragged out of the clearing by their anxious parents.

And if both boys never took their eyes off the spot Kaitlyn had previously occupied, she didn't acknowledge it to herself. She didn't dare.

As both boys would age, believing the entire experience to have been nothing more than a strange dream, they would come to wonder why their subconsciouses had 'created' a girl who looked so lonely.

<center>~~~~~~~~~</center>

Something was off.

Like, *really* off and it resulted in her incessantly pacing for days as winter decided to rear its ugly head again.

Even after hours of stewing as she paced, she couldn't decipher what it was. The Voice hadn't made a peep in over a week and the forest was livelier than she had ever remembered it being, but that couldn't have been it. This seemed bigger, like she was staring at a picture but only comprehending the small details rather than the image as a whole.

One day she lay on her side in the cave, snuggled into her sleeping bag surrounded by the wolves, scrutinizing the way the sun slowly inched above the horizon and gradually cast the frosty clearing in a glimmering pale light. She wanted to gag at the prettiness of it all.

Despite being on the move all night, she was wide awake, her racing thoughts refusing to settle. She couldn't shake the nagging feeling that something was significantly different, and her mind had taken that and ran for the hills with it. She flopped onto her back, glaring at the stone ceiling with a sour expression. She tossed and turned for another few moments, eventually settling in her original position on her side facing the mouth of the cave.

The clearing was freakin' *sparkling.*

Her left eye twitched.

'The audacity.'

She sat up so abruptly that the wolves nearest to her startled awake. Before any of them could react further, she was already picking her way over them and marching out of the cave into the chilly morning air. Her breath materialized in hazy puffs in front of her, her lungs aching with the sharp inhalations of cold. She ignored the prickle of goose bumps across her skin, striding forward with her jaw set.

115

This ended now. She hadn't slept in over 24 hours and she was going to find out what the heck was wrong if it was the last thing she ever did.

She stalked over to the outcropping of rocks she'd almost taken a swan dive off of nearly three years ago–had it really been that long? –and clambered up the stones to the top. She maintained at least a yard between her and the edge at all times. When she turned in a deliberate circle to scan her surroundings, she froze, lips parted on a silent gasp of frozen breath.

'Wait.'

She blinked her eyes rapidly, not believing them.

She looked again.

"No way," she breathed.

She was moving before she was aware of it. She leapt down the uneven rock, nearly slipping several times on icy gravel. It was a miracle she didn't twist an ankle in her haste.

Her bare feet hit the solid earth running.

'There's no way.'

She had to be dreaming.

She was moving so fast she almost didn't register the lack of sensation of moving through water as she passed from the survival spot into the barren forest.

She jerked to a stop, slowly turned around, and blinked.

She could see into the clearing.

No blurry forest mirage, no anything.

It was normal.

She dazedly reached out her hand to where the barrier should have been.

Nothing.

When had...she'd become so accustomed to the feeling that she'd failed to notice when it was gone.

'How long...? Does this mean...?' she asked herself incredulously.

She whipped around and tore through the forest like a madman, kicking up dirt and sticks and bits of detritus in her wake. The forest was a blur of brown around her as she moved without direction. She just knew she had to go somewhere, *anywhere.*

Her feet finally stopped a little while later. She bent over to rest her hands on her knees, chest heaving, panting puffs of diluted white. When she caught her breath and finally straightened, she couldn't find it in herself to be surprised when she was met with the place where it all began.

She surveyed the clearing, the grass brown and crunchy beneath her feet. She staggered back into the woods and stared. There must have been something wrong with her eyes. That, or her lack of sleep was causing her delirium. There was no way it could have taken her so long to realize it, not when it was in plain sight, when it was right in front of her nose every time she went out hunting.

She idly shuffled backward until her feet hit grass again, never once removing her gaze from the forest before her. The very *unlooped* forest.

She closed her eyes and took a few deep, steadying breaths before she opened them again.

Nothing changed.

Her knees gave out, limp body landing with a muted thump and a small rustle.

She should've felt relieved, right? Happy? Excited? Like a weight had been lifted? She should've been sprinting out of there the second she realized it. Should've already been on the road home by now, right? So why did her chest feel so heavy, why couldn't she move? Why was the only thing she could feel was this overwhelming sense of...did she dare put a name to it?

'Fear~' came a whisper of a voice along the curvature of her ear.

She flinched.

What happened to her fire? What happened to that stubborn tenacity? Why couldn't she find it? She still wanted to go back to her family, didn't she? It was the whole reason she'd fought tooth and nail all these years. The reason she'd waited The Voice out for so long. So why wasn't she seizing the opportunity right in front of her? The forest was unlooped! She could *leave! Right now!* And yet....

"So, you have finally noticed. Tch. Took you long enough."

Kaitlyn jostled to her feet, not immediately recognizing the voice she heard. It sounded worn and frayed, a shadow of something It used to be. When the familiarity of the tone clicked into place a choked noise escaped her throat, her knees threatening to bring her to the ground again. Though with the appearance of The Voice also came a transparency of the situation. The fog had cleared; she was in control.

"H-how long?" She cursed herself for the tremble in her voice but was powerless to prevent it with her scrambled nerves.

"Seven days. I was beginning to believe I would have to inform you myself."

"Why didn't you?"

A pause.

Then, *"Should you not be on your merry way back to **your pathetically wretched family by now, little girl? You survived all this time for them, so why are you still** here?"*

Not knowing the answer to that question that just moments before she had been wrestling with herself, Kaitlyn opted to dumbly state, "You didn't answer my question."

"Answer mine and I will answer yours."

She suddenly found the ground to be particularly fascinating. Maybe if she stared at it long enough she would eventually find the answer hidden in the blades of withered grass.

Time seemed to stop completely, her small world blurring together with the endless void that stretched out before her.

Why *was* she still here?

She still didn't know.

Didn't know what to do.

Didn't like that she didn't know.

It was as if she was no longer capable of forming proper reactions; she didn't know how to process that either.

She didn't know anything anymore, almost wishing the forest had remained looped so she wouldn't have had to deal with this emotional turmoil, or rather, the lack thereof. Because it felt like she was drifting aimlessly in some weird limbo. There was no direction, no objective, no anything.

"Something's wrong with me," Kaitlyn murmured softly as the world faded back into clarity.

"Perhaps," The Voice offered offhandedly.

Kaitlyn's eye involuntarily twitched.

"Gee, thanks," she spat sarcastically.

"Oh. My apologies, I was not aware you were expecting consolation. Do forgive my insolence, child."

Kaitlyn huffed at the derisive tone and sagged to the ground rather ungracefully in a cross-legged position. She propped an elbow on her knee and shoved her chin into her open hand, a scowl adorning her cracked lips.

"I don't know," she bit out, flinging out her unpreoccupied hand before letting it drop heavily.

She deflated, her body slumping as all the energy seemed to drain out of her, leaving her feeling as tired and weary as The Voice sounded. "I don't know why I'm still here," a pause, "maybe I'm waiting until you're gone before I leave."

While it was only a lackluster answer she came up with on the spot, now that she said it out loud, it made a lot of sense. It was logical. Of course she would want to ensure the Voice was gone before she left. Though part of her felt that reasoning fell short, like there was still more.

*"You **will not** be waiting long, then,"* came The Voice's raspy baritone.

"What?" flew out of Kaitlyn's mouth before she realized her tongue was forming the syllables.

*"Why must everything need to be spelled out for you, **kid? Surely you have noticed my absence, my lack of** speech within these past few fortnights."*

"Yeah but...why?" Kaitlyn found herself asking. She quickly made a sour face. Stupid mouth. She didn't care why, not at all.

'...okay maybe a little.'

The Voice released a noise that precisely conveyed just what a nuisance it thought Kaitlyn was. *"Every living **thing, be it an essence or a physical body, requires sustenance. And you, girl, you bratty pest, have been** depriving me of mine for quite some time now."*

Kaitlyn's eyebrows raised almost to her hairline as she processed the words before a complacent smirk took over her lips.

*"Do **not appear** so smug,"* The Voice spat indignantly.

The smirk fell as swiftly as it had come, replaced by a frown and furrowed eyebrows. "Wait, so you eat kids?"

The Voice snorted.

The entity sobered quickly, however. *"Souls. The more youthful they are, the better they taste."*

She wrinkled her nose. "Gross."

The Voice made a noncommittal noise.

There was a lag in conversation for a while, and when Kaitlyn finally spoke again, she half expected to be answered with silence.

"You're dying."

It wasn't a question.

A throaty sigh followed by a feathery voice, *"As your kind view it, yes."*

A strange melancholy washed over Kaitlyn. It was like-she stopped herself right there. This *Thing* wanted to *eat her*, and she nearly let herself feel sorry for It!

She contemplated her conflicting emotions. The Voice hadn't posed a genuine threat to her since she rescued Josh. The entire ordeal felt like it had transpired so long ago that it might as well have happened in an entirely different world, to an entirely different person. The emotions, the experiences, the memories were faded and threadbare. It was surreal to remember The Voice had once wished her such violent harm. But It had, and Kaitlyn needed to stop forgetting that. In the beginning It wanted her dead. It tried to kill her and just about succeeded in doing so. She had already been in a nightmare when she woke up, having realized she'd been left behind by the people who were supposed to love her, and The Voice's presence had only increased the nightmarish situation tenfold.

"You were not the first child to last longer than **expected. Though you are the first to escape me** *entirely."*

"What," she said brilliantly.

There was a gruff growl. *"I will not repeat myself."*

Kaitlyn floundered. "But–but–wait. What do you mean I wasn't the first? You said before–"

"Wicked things lie, foolish girl. **Nice things do, too. You best take heed of that."**

She grew quiet.

Then, "What happened to them?"

The Voice made a wet scoffing noise. *"I would have deemed that rather apparent."*

Kaitlyn rolled her eyes. "You know what I mean."

"Hnn~"

When The Voice failed to elaborate, Kaitlyn huffed and flopped onto her back, staring up at the little blue-gray gaps of sky between the barren branches. She shivered.

A moment later The Voice spoke again. *"Her life did not persist."*

"Stop doing all this start and stop stuff with your talking. It's annoying."

"Do you want to know or not!?" The Voice snapped unkindly.

Kaitlyn waved her hand mindlessly, adding in an eye roll because she could. "Fine, fine."

"Brat," The Voice grumbled petulantly.

'For an entity that's supposed to be really old, it sure is childish,' Kailyn remarked snidely to herself.

She stuck out her tongue.

So maybe Kaitlyn could be childish too. At least she had an excuse.

"Adorable," The Voice said in the most deadpan voice Kaitlyn had ever heard.

"Just get on with it already!" Kaitlyn whined irritably.

"She survived through the first winter with the aid of those blasted mutts, just as you did. She became wounded the following spring, however, and lacked the knowledge on plants that you possess. She contracted an infection. I suspect it moved into her blood, for it was not even a week later when she took her last breath. A shame she perished in that damnation of a survival spot. The essence is unattainable if the life passes within those barriers; it was an unfortunate waste."

Kaitlyn allowed herself a moment to process. Another girl had died in the same survival spot she'd been living in for the past few years. She was left behind by her parents too, likely possessed the same hope she herself did that they would one day return to her. There was some solace in the fact that this other girl never had to face the bitter reality. That she never had to know The Voice made them forget her. At least she didn't have to unwillingly accept that if she'd wanted to see her parents again, she would've had to go to them herself. The only thing that kept

Kaitlyn from mourning too deeply about the loss of a girl she'd never met was that The Voice hadn't succeeded in consuming her, that she'd had the wolves to support her. It was better than nothing at all.

Kaitlyn glared up at the naked tree branches. Her hands fisted tightly in the dead grass, her jaw clenching painfully. "I'm glad you didn't get to eat her Scratchy Voice, I'm glad you didn't get to eat *me,* and I'm glad that you're dying," she said with venomous conviction.

*"Yes, it **appears that** you are."*

Maybe it was merely her wishful thinking, but she swore The Voice sounded fainter than before.

'Shouldn't be long now,' Kaitlyn thought to herself.

Still glaring, she added, "That means I win y'know."

"Does it now~?" The Voice mocked thinly.

She sat up, hands continuing to tightly fist the grass in a white-knuckle grip. "Yeah. You're dying, and I'm still alive. I'll be leaving once you're gone."

The Voice released a bout of hacking laughter that made Kaitlyn cringe. ***"Foolish*** *human girl,"* It drawled slowly in a dangerously unhinged lilt, *"Are you certain? Have you* ***forgotten your parents will not recognize you? In their eyes, you would be a mere stranger, an intruder in their happy little lives. To the rest of the world, you. Do not. Exist. You are nothing. Nothing is all you will ever be."***

An icy, phantom hand clamped around Kaitlyn's throat and squeezed. Her gut twisted; her spine seized up.

"Y-you–you could be lying. You s-said so...yourself," she gritted out in a strained voice.

The Voice scoffed wetly. The sound seemed to break the spell that had bewitched her. She grasped at her throat, inhaling deeply. There had been nothing there, yet it had felt so real.

"I will be gone soon enough, brat. I have no more reason left to lie to you regarding such menial things."

"You don't scare me anymore, Scratchy Voice. You haven't

scared me in a long time. I'm still going to try. No matter what you say, there's still a chance that they'll remember. I won't give up," said Kaitlyn with quiet firmness.

"You won but a meager battle based solely upon luck. **Perhaps I lost to you here, but I believe we are both** *aware who triumphed in this war."*

She bit her lip to stifle the guffaw that wanted to burst forth, saying. "Right. *Okay.*"

A soft whistle floated through the air, twining around the branches as it crept over the frosted earth. *"I would* **not feel so pleased. Real evil never truly dies, Kaitlyn. It** *simply retreats, and then comes back stronger."*

The change was immediate. The air around her was lighter, fresher, as if the forest had been thoroughly cleansed.

She knew The Voice was gone, though she still shifted uneasily where she sat. She disliked the implications of those parting words, did her best to refrain from overthinking them. If she didn't acknowledge it, then it didn't exist, right?

'So why am I still freaking sitting here then?'

With that in mind, she scrambled to her feet and started sprinting in the direction she thought she remembered the parking lot being in.

It was almost unsettling to be running through the forest by herself. She'd grown so accustomed to being accompanied by at least one wolf wherever she went that she nearly forgot what it was like to be alone. There was an internal voice setting off alarm bells screeching, "Wrong! Wrong! *Wrong!*"

Time seemed to become intangible as she navigated her way through the forest. She was all too aware of the distinct thumps and cracks of her bare feet pounding the frozen earth, all too aware of her own heart beating too loud in her ears.

She soaked in the new landscape. The differences were subtle, but she gawked at her surroundings like she'd never seen a forest before. It was surreal. It felt like a dream.

She found herself smiling a little. A slight curling up of the ends of her lips.

A few minutes of jogging later, she saw slivers of dark gray and flashes of sunshine yellow through the thinning trees.

She ran faster, practically slipping on particularly icy patches of ground as she went.

She exploded from the trees in a frenzy of wild hair, dead branches and flailing limbs, crossing abruptly from dirt to rough pavement. She gasped harshly, lungs stinging, exhaling plumes of chilled winter breath.

Plain, old, man-made concrete had never looked so beautiful.

She was out.

After a little over three agonizing years of torture and enough near-death experiences for a hundred lifetimes, she was finally out. Finally free.

The parking lot was empty, appearing as she vaguely remembered it. There was a wide gravel pathway on the far side of the lot that supposedly led to the main road, and there onward, home.

'Home!'

Without a backward glance, she began her trek across the parking lot with a little hop in her step. The winter chill was no more than a tickle on her skin, felt no sensation of the cold attempting to seep through the thick, tough pads of her feet. She'd get on the main road and follow the signs back to her hometown, Forest Grove. From there she'd be able to navigate the way to her house from a somewhat unreliable memory. After that, she'd have to play it by ear. Though not even the fear of the unknown was enough to deter her. Because she was *out.* She finally made it!

She'd barely taken a dozen steps before a thought stopped her rigid in her tracks. It was almost as if a fraction of her brain was tethered to a string attached to a location deep in the woods at her back.

'What if The Voice comes back?'

She didn't need this. She didn't *want* this. Where'd the thought even come from? Why now, when she was so *close!?*

So *what* if The Voice came back? That wasn't her problem anymore!

'What about the kids to come?'

'They'll be fine,' she tried to reason with herself.

But she knew they wouldn't. It was unlikely The Voice would return at all, and even if It did, it probably wouldn't be for a long time...but was she really willing to take that chance? The Voice could have easily faked everything back there, attempting to trick her into the false belief that It was gone so she would leave. If The Voice did return, she wouldn't have any way of knowing. All the kids that would die...but what about her family? Of course she wanted to go back to them, but The Voice claimed they didn't remember. While It could have been lying about that too, if her parents did remember her, then surely they would have come to retrieve her by now. And how likely was it for her to force them to remember? Was she willing to take *that* chance? It was a path involving a lot of blind faith, faith Kaitlyn wasn't entirely certain she possessed anymore.

She could always go home, try and make her family remember, and if her efforts proved unsuccessful, she could come back...

But somehow, she knew that if she left, she wouldn't be able to bring herself to return to this place.

She couldn't overlook the wolves either. Was she willing to relinquish the bond they'd establish over something that wasn't guaranteed? They'd filled in the empty spaces her old family members had once resided, and she found herself reluctant to let her canine friends go when they were the ones who had been there for her. At least if she stayed, then she could ensure The Voice remained gone and that no more souls would be 'eaten.' She *had* a family here, one that was loyal and nurturing. She could keep others safe by staying here, and if her family didn't remember her anyway, then they weren't missing her, right? They weren't in pain. If she unceremoniously barged back into their lives, lives they were living blissfully unaware that she was once part of, then it would only create a hassle with potential police intervention. She'd likely end up in a nut house or a foster home. No one needed that. If they had enough will power, they should have been capable of remembering on their own by now. The Voice made it clear that Its departure didn't automatically mean the damage It caused was undone, so Kaitlyn's family presumably didn't suddenly get their memories back just because The Voice 'died.'

She weighed her options. Stay in the forest with the wolves and keep The Voice away while simultaneously saving who knows how many lives in the process? Or leave to return to a home that would likely view you as an unwelcome stranger in a place you once rested your head, having to stare into cold eyes that once beheld you with warmth?

For Kaitlyn, the choice was obvious, though that didn't make it any easier to stomach.

She hated logic. She really did.

She collapsed to the ground, ignoring the stings of pain she felt stab at her knees and shins. She stared desolately at the road across the lot that mere minutes ago, she was so certain she was going to go down.

Her vision blurred, wet trails bleeding down her wind bitten cheeks. A hand curled into a fist and weakly beat the pavement only once. A head bowed, short, tangled, auburn hair shifting to shadow a pair of anguished, blue-green eyes.

A single tear rolled off a chin and fell to cold stone.

The same pair of blue-green eyes fluttered closed, squeezed once before softening. Defeated.

"...Dang it."

CHAPTER NINE

"**I** hate you."

The redhead guffawed at the other male's comment, carelessly kicking the car door closed and sauntering around to the driver's side to open it.

It was locked.

Pursing his lips, the teen pointedly tapped a finger on the glass window. When the boy inside merely raised a dark eyebrow and made a show of turning his attention to his phone, the ginger threw his head back with a groan.

"Come on Wes! You do this every time! It'll be fun, you'll see," the teen all but whined.

Wes cast his eyes heavenward before reluctantly unlocking the door and letting himself out. He did so so suddenly that the corner of the door rammed itself into the other boy's knee, causing him to double over, clutching at it as he hopped on one foot.

Wes blinked.

"Whoops," he offered with a shrug.

Still muttering a rather creative slew of curses under his breath, the redhead glared up at Wes.

Righting himself, he punched the other boy in the arm, "You're such an ass," yet there was a smile on his face.

Wes batted his eyes. "Only for you, *Rivera*."

River made a face like he'd just smelled something rotten. "Keep calling me that, and I'll never bring you with me to one of these things again."

"I'm your driver. You wouldn't even be here if it weren't

"

for me," Wes retorted with a simpering grin as he started sauntering toward the large house that loomed before them.

"You don't have to, y'know. No one's forcing you," River muttered petulantly, jogging to catch up.

Wes playfully rolled his dark eyes. "Someone has to keep an eye on you," he cooed. "We don't want a repeat of 'The Incident.'"

River's mouth curled wickedly. "You act like you weren't part of it."

Feigning ignorance, Wes made a flippant gesture with his hand. "I've no idea what you mean."

River tugged on Wes's ear. "Bite me, Wes."

Wes paused, turning to look at River, appraising him as if considering it.

Eventually he said, "Nah. Not a fan of carrots."

River's mouth fell open as he stopped in his tracks, watching his smart-mouthed friend continue through the neatly trimmed grass toward the house. Wes glanced over his shoulder, snickering to himself with a wicked gleam in his eye.

Snapping out of it, River shook himself and went running after him, grabbing Wes's wrist to tug him to a stop. "I'm sorry, what was that?"

Avoiding eye contact while trying to suppress a smile, Wes half-heartedly attempted to free his hand. "You heard me. Or does all that Red 40 in your hair inhibit your hearing too?"

An incredulous laugh burst out of River, "Hoh! You should try cleaning all that crap off your face, Freckles. Maybe then you might be able to get a girl to actually talk to you."

Wes snorted, "You're one to talk. When's the last time a girl talked to you? Hmm?"

River faltered, dropping Wes's wrist before he piped up, "There was that one time–wait, no, that was a dude who looked like a girl. But last week I–well, I initiated that one, and she told me to shove it...Oh! What about–"

Wes's hand slapping River's back cut him off, Wes turning to look at his friend solemnly. "Face it, River. The two of us are just meant to die alone," he said with a wistful sigh as he leaned his head on his friend's shoulder.

River mimicked the sigh, dramatically letting his own head rest on Wes's. "At least we—"

The mahogany front door of the absurdly large house opened abruptly, interrupting him, a steady throb of EDM music vibrating out into the night from the rooms within. A girl with generous facial piercings and deep violet hair leaned lazily on the ornate doorframe with her arms crossed.

After a short pause of pinning them with an unimpressed stare, she drawled, "Do you two plan on coming in any time soon, or are you just going to have your weird ass foreplay on my lawn all night?"

The two boys shared a side-eye from where their heads rested on each other, slow smirks simultaneously spreading their lips. The girl scoffed through her nose, shaking her head as she retreated into the house, leaving the door ajar.

"Nice to see you too, Dylan!" River called after her.

A pale hand reappeared in the door giving a one finger salute.

Wes nodded his head in a feign of approval. "Nice."

Rolling his eyes, River grabbed his best friend's arm and dragged him into the darkened house. On their way, Wes caught a brief sight of an elaborate chandelier hanging above the door before it was closed in his stead. He was met with another ornate chandelier, this one even more sparkly than the last, in the parlor they'd just entered; his lip curled up in mild distaste.

'Damn rich people,' he thought to himself.

River led him further into the house, the parlor giving way to a spacious sitting room, occupied by a sweaty, drunk, undulating mass of teenagers bathed in multi-colored disco lights.

Wes's lip curled even further. He could see red solo cups held aloft in the air, the hardwood floor slick with condensation and who knew what else.

He took another simpering look at the sea of 'ew' and promptly made his attempt at escape.

River's grip held strong, however, and Wes groaned as the other male grinned back at him with a devious gleam in his blue eyes. "You'll have to be more subtle than that," Wes barely heard him say over the deafening music.

Wes made a face at River when his back was turned, reluctantly allowing himself to be led further into the stifling room, not that he had much of a choice.

They eventually found themselves in the kitchen, the kitchen and its polished marble countertops, numerous shiny appliances, and meticulously embroidered curtains. The sheer status everything in this house exuded made Wes want to throw himself off the third story balcony he'd seen when they'd pulled up.

River poured them both drinks; Wes took one whiff of his and instantly dumped it in the sink. He eyed the other male as he took a gulp, and upon catching his stare, River shrugged and continued drinking.

"Didn't Josh say he was coming?" Wes asked after a moment.

"What!?" River shouted.

Wes grabbed River's shoulders and yanked him in as close as physically possible before repeating himself in his ear, "*Didn't Josh say he was coming?!*"

River jerked back, rubbing his ear against his shoulder. "Sheesh, no need to yell."

Wes blinked.

River held his hands up with a sheepish smile. "Kidding. But yeah, I think he did say. Who knows where he's ended up though. You know how he is."

Wes did know how Josh was, and he lost track of the number of times he had to bail him out of sticky situations once the count passed the capabilities of his fingers.

He gave a long-suffering sigh. "Come on, we should go find him. And would you quit drinking that?" he scolded as he grabbed the cup and threw it in the trash.

"It's good though," River protested as he followed Wes back into the sea of sweat.

"It's also probably spiked to hell and back."

"Even better!" River chirped.

Wes shook his head but gave no further response. River knew he wasn't too mad though, given the small upturn he caught on his friend's lips.

When they couldn't find Josh on the bottom floor, and had no luck with the generously furnished basement, they headed up the stairs, side-stepping a couple playing tonsil hockey on the landing. With a miniscule scrunch of his nose, Wes attempted to keep his expression schooled into one of apathy, but River's mock gagging sounds behind him made the task a rather difficult feat.

A few minutes of searching later, they came upon the third story balcony Wes had seen earlier, and just as they were about to open the door, it was already swinging open with enough force to break someone's nose. Next thing either of them knew, Miranda Harris, a petite raven haired "It" girl in their grade, came huffing into the hall. Her heels clapping obnoxiously on the polished wood floor, she resembled an angry Pomeranian as she stormed past them without a backward glance.

Sharing a stunned look, they both stuck their heads out into the cool night air, finding a dejected Josh, in all his blond glory, who was gazing mournfully into his mostly full cup.

They approached him, River clapping him on the shoulder and asking, "What'd you say *this* time?"

"Nothin'!" the blond burst.

Wes raised an eyebrow.

"...Well, I told her her outfit was nice but kinda loud and how I thought she was wearing too much makeup because it looked like a mask. I also said caking it on like that wasn't going to win Jared back and that I'd be happy to take her out for coffee tomorrow to help her get over him..."

Both teens stared blankly at their friend, Wes's lips having parted in slight incredulity.

"She asked! I was just being honest," Josh defended himself, spilling some of his drink in the process of his upset.

"I swear, your lack of brain to mouth filter is going to get you slapped someday," River admonished with a sympathetic shoulder pat.

"Too late..." Josh grumbled so low they almost didn't hear him.

"Josh, sometimes honesty isn't the best policy. Especially when you're dealing with someone like Miranda Harris, of all people. Why were you even talking to her anyway?" Wes asked.

Josh scowled. "Dylan."

River laughed earnestly. "Why am I not surprised?"

They all fell into easy conversation for a while, flowing from one absurd topic to the next. The cool night air was relaxing; it felt like their little balcony was part of a separate world from the churning abyss below. Sometime into the night, Dylan stuck her head through the high archway that led out onto the balcony, asking if they, losers, wanted to come and swim, as she decided to open up the hot tub and pool since a lot of the underclassmen had gone home.

Wes glanced at his watch, eyes widening upon noticing how late it had gotten. Josh nodded his affirmative and Wes gave his too. When Dylan turned to River, the redhead waved her off.

"I'll pass. I don't have anything to swim in anyway."

"Dude, just go in your boxers," Josh pointed out.

At River's stubborn silence, a Cheshire grin split Wes's face. "You're wearing them, aren't you?"

When River responded with a warning glare and bit out a, "Shut up," Wes's smile morphed into one of pure glee.

Josh's expression transformed into understanding before he blew his cheeks out to keep from laughing. "Guess you weren't planning on gettin' any tonight, huh, bud?"

River made to elbow him, but Josh scantly evaded with a simpering grin.

Dylan's eyes narrowed. "Wearing what?"

"His—" but Josh was cut off by River's hand slapping over his mouth.

"Nothing," River said firmly.

He turned on Wes when he saw him bite his lip, wiggling his eyebrows as his form bounced giddily. "Don't you dare."

"The heart ones his mom got him for Valentine's Day," Wes rushed out.

"Dammit Wes!" River burst in irritation.

Dylan looked on with amusement. "They come with a box of chocolates and a teddy bear, too?"

River shot her a dirty look, to which she only smirked back at him with obvious relish at his predicament.

He then turned pointedly to a snickering Wes who looked far too pleased with himself. "You're a real sadist, you know that?"

Wes inclined his head. "And?"

"I hate you all," River deadpanned.

Dylan scoffed. "You love us. Come on, you can borrow a pair of my brother's swim shorts if you want. He won't care."

River sighed with relief. Dylan made it as if she was about to turn around but appeared to think better of it at the last second.

"And River?"

"Yeah?" he replied.

"You're suffocating Josh," she finished in an overtly somber voice, picking at her polished black nails with disinterest.

River immediately snatched his hand from Josh's mouth as if he'd been burned. Josh abruptly sucked in a deep breath, placing one hand on the railing and one on his knee to steady himself.

"Why didn't you just breathe through your nose!?" River yelped in distress.

Huffing and puffing and head bowed, Josh choked out, "You...were covering...that too."

Dylan sucked in an exasperated breath, "Drama queens. Let's go, before I decide to kick you out."

Then she was gone, leaving the three boys alone on the shadowed balcony. They all shared a dorky look before moving to follow her.

~~~~~~~~~

"Not the hair, not the hair, not the hair!" Josh screeched as he wrapped his arms around his head.

"Whoo! Jacuuuu-zii!" Was all the warning the five teenagers received before River hit the water with a colossal splash.

When he resurfaced, he was met with a cacophony of disgruntled complaints and annoyed groans.

Josh's glare of imminent death from behind his sopping bangs looked like a waterlogged puppy trying to imitate an angry doberman, which only added to River's delight.

Once everyone settled down, River glanced around at the new faces of the night. Of course, Dylan, Josh and Wes were there, but there were also two other girls, who he vaguely recalled were identical twins, Sarah and Amy. Both had midnight hair; the one with bouncy, corkscrew
~~~~~~~~~

curls was all smiles and giggles while the one with pin-straight hair looked like she had a bone to pick with life, shoulders high and a haughty stare.

'Yeesh, what crawled inside her and died?' he thought to himself, pressing his back more firmly against the plastic backing of the hot tub.

River zoned out for a while, narrowly aware of the sound of Dylan and Josh bickering. He shared the occasional idle stare with Wes until he saw that his friend's eyes had gradually drifted close. River almost purposely elbowed him in the ribs to get him back for the door earlier, but quickly changed his mind.

'I'm takin' the high road,' he thought snootily to himself, crossing his arms with a satisfied little 'hmph.'

'For once,' his subconscious supplied unhelpfully.

River's scathing inner dialogue was interrupted when the curly haired twin suddenly turned to Dylan with excessive exuberance. "Okay, truth or dare?"

River saw Wes crack an eye open out of the corner of his own eye.

"Really?" Dylan droned.

Rapidly poking her arm with unnecessary force, Sarah urged, "Answer the question."

Dylan grasped the girl's wrist to stop its incessant motion.

"Ow," she voiced deliberately.

When 'Curly' just peered at her without remorse in response, Dylan bit out an exasperated, "Fine."

And so, the cliché teenage party game went, becoming more ludicrous the deeper they traversed into the night. River's personal favorite was when Dylan dared Josh to snort water out his nose and Josh actually going through with it when promised all of Dylan's leftover party snacks.

River eventually learned 'Curly' was Sarah, and when it was his turn to ask a question, he turned to her. "Truth or dare?"

"Truth," she chirped.

He thought for a moment, and eventually, Wes leaned over and whispered something in his ear.

River snapped his fingers. "What's the weirdest dream you've ever had?"

Cupping her hands over her mouth, Dylan called, "Boor-ring!"

"You're boring!" Josh parried.

"Wow, clever," Dylan drawled with feigned awe.

Grimacing, Amy said, "Real mature guys."

"No one asked you!" They both proclaimed in unison.

Amy held up her hands, eyes wide.

"Oh," Sarah exclaimed, displacing water in her excitement.

All eyes on her, she continued, "Our parents took me and Amy camping when we were younger, out at Timber Point. The first night we stayed there-the only night really, I dreamed about standing outside our tent and seeing this girl in front of our parents. She was really wild looking, had messy hair and wore animal skins. I didn't see much else before she ran into the woods, then I woke up outside the tent. Apparently, I'd been sleep walking. Our parents made us pack up immediately though, and now that I think about it, the whole thing seemed kind of strange...."

As Sarah trailed off, she failed to realize the way everyone else had fallen eerily silent. The wind suddenly intensified, making goosebumps erupt down River's exposed arms.

His head shot up when Josh's uncharacteristically quiet voice fractured the uneasy stillness of the night. "I had the same dream, when I went there."

Wes's head tipped back as he gazed absently up at the full moon. "I did too," he spoke softly, sounding as if he'd retreated far away.

River glanced over at him sharply, his blue eyes flashing silver in the pale moonlight.

His heart rate sped up, and when Wes's head drifted back down, pinning him in place with those dark eyes of his,

River suddenly recalled the lonely wild girl he'd seen in the forest when he was 11 years old, the girl he forced himself to write off as being wrought from his childish imagination.

"Yeah," slipped from his lips. Sand in an hourglass. Time trickling away into deep mahogany. Grain by grain.

River lost himself in those eyes for a moment. He quickly shook himself, disconnecting from the soulful stare.

"Amy? Dylan?" Josh questioned softly.

Amy wrapped her arms tightly around herself, nodding mutely.

Dylan ran a troubled hand through her hair, looking more frazzled than River had ever seen her before.

"This is getting weird," she breathed.

"So..." Sarah began uncertainly, "we all went camping out at Timber Point, and we all had the same dream. Did you guys leave the first night, too?"

They all nodded.

Quiet befell them, the only sound heard was the bubbling of the hot tub jets. River skimmed his hand over the surface of the churning water, trying to make the new information fit into a picture that made sense.

"What if it wasn't a dream?" shattered the strained silence.

It was blurted with the kind of finesse that implied the speaker hadn't really meant to say it out loud.

Everyone looked at Josh.

Sarah cocked her head to the side, damp midnight curls plastering to the delicate curve of her neck. "What do you mean?"

Josh shifted minutely, looking hesitant and unsettled. "I mean, I don't know. I just—it can't be a coincidence that we all had a dream about the same place with the same girl under the exact same circumstances. It just doesn't add up like that."

Dylan stared at him in mock awe. "Wow Joshy, I think that's the smartest thing you've ever said."

Josh rolled his blue eyes. "I'm serious. What if there's actually a girl out in those woods?"

Amy scoffed. "Don't be daft. The probability of someone, let alone a child, surviving out in the wilderness by themselves, without appropriate resources and skills, is slim to none. They'd either die of malnutrition, infection, exposure, dehydration, or get mauled by some animal."

"Okay, if you're so smart, then explain why we all had the same dream in the same place." Josh crossed his arms, raising both his eyebrows in defiance.

Amy narrowed her gray eyes. "Well..." She then proceeded to launch into a long-winded and detailed theory of dream synchronization to which everyone immediately tuned out.

"What if we went out there?" River asked, not realizing he'd spoken aloud until he became aware of five pairs of eyes boring into him.

He hastened to explain himself. "I just mean that we won't know anything for sure unless we check ourselves. There's really no harm in going out there."

"We can leave this weekend. Take a camping trip for a week," Wes offered easily.

River turned to him in surprise, not expecting Wes to be so quick to entertain the idea, let alone jump on board with it.

Dylan stretched her arms over her head, a series of pops resounding from her arched spine. "You two can go. Like hell I'm sleeping in the dirt."

"What if she's dangerous?" Sarah asked, worrying her bottom lip.

Dylan appeared unconvinced. "I doubt it. Don't you remember how scrawny she looked? What's to say she was even out there at all? On the off chance she was there, she might be dead now."

Sarah flinched at the last part and Dylan's lack of finesse, refusing to think about it. "But still...."

"I'm not going," Amy declared. "I'm not chasing the idea of a girl whose existence is next to impossible."

"You'd just be a stick in the mud, anyway," Josh muttered, ignoring Amy's dirty look.

Then to River and Wes. "My parents are taking me to go see some local colleges this weekend, so I can't come."

"And I'm not going if Amy's not," Sarah added in, though she didn't look pleased.

Turning to Wes. "Looks like it's just you and me then," River stated, sticking his hand out for a fist-bump.

Wes stared blankly at the outstretched hand, making no move to return the gesture.

"Come on man, don't leave me hanging!" River whined.

Rolling his eyes, Wes reluctantly tapped his fist against River's, muttering exasperatedly, "You're such a child."

River shoved Wes's shoulder, and Wes shoved him right back, splashing water over the side of the hot tub onto the cement floor.

Eventually, a full out war erupted between the six of them, the wild girl all but forgotten.

But later that night while driving home, River noticed Wes's eyes still held remnants of disturbance. He knew Wes wasn't completely present, staring off at something beyond the road he himself was incapable of seeing. He always felt helpless when his friend got like this, as he often retreated into his own mind, a place where River couldn't go.

He placed a hand briefly on Wes's forearm where it rested on the steering wheel, not registering the resulting startled response he received from the gesture. He allowed his hand to slide down the other male's arm and slip from his elbow before he resignedly rested his temple on the car's cool passenger window, eyes fluttering closed.

River would never know it, but the corners of Wes's lips twitched up, and he returned from that place River was supposedly incapable of reaching.

CHAPTER TEN
THE ARRIVAL

Five years. Five years since The Voice had gone, the forest returned to its rightful normality. Five years since she decided to stay.

She was 18 now, the age many often wished their years away waiting to become.

The number held no precedence in Kaitlyn's life. It didn't matter. It didn't matter how old she was or how many years had passed, or what she looked like. What mattered was she was alive, she was well...and she was happy. Happier than she ever recalled being.

It had taken her longer than she cared to admit to realize that once she'd finally let go of her old life, the weight on her shoulders began to lighten. She was no longer anchored down to a past that didn't care to remember her, no longer stuck on an idea that wasn't worth the energy to expend. As soon as she released her vice grip on everything back in her hometown of Forest Grove, it was like emerging on the other side of a thick, suffocating fog and taking the first breath of fresh air she'd had in years.

She would always miss what she once had, what she would never have again, but not enough to trade it in for what she'd gained and what she had *now.*

This vast expanse of beautifully wild forest all to herself and her canine family. No Scratchy Voice around to torment her, no naive dreams of returning to the place she once called home to plague her mind and siphon her energy. Because she *was* home. This forest, the one she used to curse for its very existence, was her home now.

This was where she belonged, out here in the wilderness where she could be whoever she wanted to be, where there were no limits.

Maybe it was lonely sometimes, and maybe there was a gaping wound inside her that throbbed with a distant pain and oozed around the haphazard stitches when she found herself lying awake in the middle of the night. Maybe she still had dreams that left her chest tight and her throat closing up when she startled awake. Maybe those scars aimlessly slashing across her body still ached when the days grew cold. But unlike what The Voice once maintained, she wasn't alone. She had the wolves, she had the forest and all the animals that dwelled within it, and she had herself.

That had to be enough.

It's not like she had another option.

<center>~~~~~~~~~</center>

"Let's go Midnight! You're not *actually* scared of a little water, are you?" a slightly gravelly female voice taunted.

There was an answering bark that if one strained their ears, they might have been able to hear the indignant undertones.

"Then come on already!"

The girl ran ahead up the path, her short auburn hair a wild mane behind her, her feet blurs as they raced the ground. When she peaked at the top of the incline, she skidded to a gradual halt, gazing out over the ledge at the sparkling blue water and the lively forest beyond. She scented the air, detecting the faintest traces of earth that hinted at the incoming approach of fall, felt the cold spray from the waterfall off to her right.

A few moments later a great, hulking black mass trotted up behind her.

Without turning around, the girl, Kaitlyn, retorted, "Took you long enough."

142

An affronted snort was the only reply she received.

She snorted back and turned around to face the wolf, placing her hands firmly on narrow hips.

"We're going to jump," she stated, chin inclined.

Midnight blinked at her.

She continued, "We're going to jump and it's going to be fun and you'll thank me later."

The wolf yawned.

Heaving a long-suffering sigh, she backed up to the ledge, and with a loud and joyous *whoop!* launched herself in a backflip off the rocks, plummeting in a graceful arc to the crystal blue water below. The splash that followed was completely lost to the deafening roar of the waterfall. The girl surfaced a few moments later with a grin adorning her chapped lips.

She kicked up until she was floating on her back, the sun casting her in its golden halo. She then turned her cyan gaze up to the place she'd recently jumped from and saw a furry black head peering over the edge; her smile growing a little more wolfish.

A moment later there was a series of shrill yips before two fluffy, dark gray blurs blazed past Midnight and came hurtling over the edge.

Twin splashes sounded off to her left, and just as the ripples began to smooth, two heads popped out of the water, tongues lolling happily.

Kaitlyn shot Midnight a wickedly knowing look. "You really gonna let your own pups show you up?"

The wolf's striking blue eyes seemed to narrow before she sniffed, turned around, and disappeared from view. Before Kaitlyn could lift a hand to pat herself on the back for a job well done, the canine was leaping over the edge, hitting the water with a loud clap.

A drenched, inky black head resurfaced immediately, resembling a drowned rat.

Kaitlyn bit her lip and puffed out her cheeks in an

attempt to prevent her laughter.

"Pfffff."

Then Midnight was lunging at Kaitlyn, wet paws and tongue closing in on her face with impending doom. Kaitlyn managed to duck out of the way of the imminent wet dog smell just in time, the fact being supported by the tickle of fur across her cheek.

Without looking back, she started to swim away at the sounds of splashing behind her. However, she couldn't help herself for long and snuck a peek over her shoulder. She reeled back with a high-pitched squeal upon seeing how close Midnight and her pups were on her tail.

Thud.

They all froze.

The three wolves and the human lifted their heads to the wind.

Thud.

There it was again. A faint, hollow, metallic sound from off in the distance. It sounded familiar to Kaitlyn, almost nostalgic in a way. She'd heard that noise before. An echo of a past forcefully forgotten. Such a painfully bittersweet sound that she felt something crack inside her.

The three wolves slowly made their way to the shore, Kaitlyn purposefully following further behind. Once they all arrived, Midnight and her pups shook themselves briefly and went to join the rest of their pack, leaving Kaitlyn standing by the lake, drenched and alone. She was shaking in a way one might associate with being freezing cold, but the breeze was warm, the sun was glaring down at her. She hugged her arms tightly around her torso, watching idly as the wolves crept past the treeline and disappeared into the sun dappled forest.

She reluctantly made her way to the edge of the woods, thoroughly squishing out her dress and hair as she went. She suppressed the feeling from a few moments ago. She didn't know why she was so rattled. It was just a stupid noise, probably made by a bird or something.

She slapped herself lightly on the cheeks. "You're being ridiculous," she told herself aloud.

Then she took off silently into the forest, her feet traveling across the ground as if she were a ghost.

And maybe, in some sense of the term, she was.

~~~~~~~~~~

"Uuuuggh! Wes, how much longer?" River griped over the quiet beat of radio pop music, head lolling back on the dark leather headrest.

Unperturbed, with hands placed firm and steady on the steering wheel, Wes responded, "Five minutes."

"Really?"

"No."

"Sadist."

Wes grinned, briefly glancing at River out of the corner of his eye. "What kind of best friend would I be if I didn't push your buttons?"

Looking out the slightly tinted window at the world blurring by, River pouted. "A good one."

"Oh darling, how you wound me so."

River rolled his eyes playfully, a small smile on his face. "Okay shitface. But seriously, how much longer?"

A thoughtfully reminiscent look on his face, Wes replied, "Still not a fan of long car rides, huh?"

River huffed, moodily staring out the front windshield with his arms crossed. "It's not so bad anymore, I'm just impatient."

Smirking lightly, Wes took a left turn with ease and said, "You said it, not me–and 10 minutes."

River glanced over at him, slim brows furrowed. "Huh?"

"Until we get there," Wes added, his smirk growing.

River smacked his forehead. "Oh, doi."

"...Pfft."
~~~~~~~~~~

River whipped his head toward Wes, his hands smacking his jean clad thighs and appearing mildly offended. "Don't laugh at my vocabulary!"

"What's a doi?"

"Shut up," the redhead grumbled, hunching into the seat.

Silence.

River visibly relaxed, even humming along quietly to the radio.

"You pick up that one up from Josh?"

"Dammit Wesley!"

The only response was Wes's boisterous laughter as they drove down the tree-shaded road.

~~~~~~~~~~

A car door slammed.

"Ugh, we were in that car for hours!" River complained as he stretched his arms over his head.

A second car door slammed.

"It wasn't even two, and you call me dramatic," Wes countered as he eyed him from the opposite side of the shiny chrome front hood. Wes then rounded to the back of the car and used his fob to pop the trunk.

River followed suit, elbowing Wes good naturedly in the side as he came to stand beside him. "You *are* dramatic," he emphasized with a simpering grin.

Wes looked at him for a second, making a variety of peculiar faces like he didn't know what to say before settling on: "I hope you stub your toe on a rock."

He proceeded to lift the back hood and sling a duffle bag over each shoulder.

The ginger male guffawed loudly and did the same. As he came up beside his best friend, his eyes lit up.

Wes saw River pause out of the corner of his eye, and was about to turn and ask what he was doing before his
~~~~~~~~~~

friend yelled, "Race you to the trail!" and took off in a dead sprint, duffle bags bouncing off his form with reckless abandon as he went.

Wes rose to the challenge at once, a wolfish grin taking over his tanned face as he chased after River, his sneakered feet pounding the worn pavement, the sound echoing through the parking lot.

River reached the trailhead first, releasing a loud, gleeful *Whoop!* when he did, finishing with a dorky little victory jig.

Wes wasn't far behind though, rolling his eyes when he arrived. His breath was coming in quiet huffs. River, on the other hand, had barely broken a sweat.

Wes narrowed his eyes, but they were swimming with mirth. "You only won 'cause you got a head start."

River, still teeming with his victory, turned around to face him. "Maybe you're just a sore loser," he sang out.

Wes snorted, waving a hand airily, "Please, you run track...and cross country. I don't. It's simple logic."

River looked like he was trying not to laugh.

River raised an eyebrow (or at least tried to, since he wasn't very good at it), a teasing expression on his face. "And whose fault is that? Coach has been trying to get you on the team since Freshman year." He nudged Wes with his shoulder.

But Wes wasn't listening to him anymore, his attention directed into the forest that opened up before them. A light breeze rustled the branches, lifting strands of his hair like feathers on a wind current. He had that look on his face again, eyes suddenly vacated as he stared off into the spaces between the trees. River followed his gaze, and while he couldn't see anything out of order, he felt a brief wave of despair wash over him. It was gone as soon as it had come, leaving River to wonder where the hell it had come from. When he regained his bearings, he found Wes staring at him with this unfathomable look.

"Come on," River murmured, sidling past his friend as he crossed from that which was man-made, into the land of the wild.

~~~~~~~~~

What.

Just, *what?*

Kaitlyn dragged her hands down her face before looking back at the scene in front of her.

It hadn't changed. Why hadn't it changed!? This should've been a dream. There was no way this was real, that *they* were real.

She dug her nails into the flesh of her upper arms from their crossed position., scarcely refraining from making a pained noise. Nope. Not a dream. Abort mission! Abort— she took a deep breath.

'Pull yourself together,' she chided herself.

She glanced at Midnight only to find her, as well as the rest of the pack, slinking back into the foliage and out of sight.

Kaitlyn was left gaping at the spot where they had previously resided. Collecting herself, she scowled as she made a mental note to give them all the silent treatment for leaving her to handle this *completely impossible* situation. *By herself.* Ugh. No one had come to these woods in years. Five years to be exact, or rather, ever since she started saving those kids. Now that she thought about it, the two boys in front of her looked vaguely familiar— No. She didn't want to think about it. She just wanted them to leave. She was perfectly happy with her life here. It was her own little bubble of paradise that sheltered her from the world where she no longer existed. The appearance of the two males before her were dangerously close to exhuming things she would rather keep buried deep within the earth.
~~~~~~~~~

Memories of a life since gone, of voices since faded, and people since turned to faceless strangers. She hadn't realized until now just how much she had forgotten what another human looked like. Sure, she had herself, had seen her appearance and development reflected back at her from too clear water from a too pretty lake, but it was *her*. She was used to *her*. This, these boys, were not something she was used to. How long were they even planning on staying? Whatever the answer to that was, it would be too long.

She glanced around helplessly, at a loss of what to do.

Did she ignore them and hope they didn't stumble upon her home? Did she confront them and demand they leave? Well, that probably wouldn't end too well, so the confrontation option was out.

'Hmm, maybe I can take another approach,' she thought to herself.

Maybe she could freak them out so much that she could chase them back to where they came from without even needing to show herself. Yeah. Yeah, that could definitely work. There was only one problem.

'Just how am I supposed to do that!?'

She buried her hands in her still damp hair, feeling her fingers catch in multiple tangles. She started to pace back and forth just beyond the treeline of the small clearing, occasionally glancing up when she heard boisterous laughter or a curse of frustration. Every time the one boy did so, birds would scatter from the nearby trees and the other dark-haired boy would shoot him a look that fell midway between fond amusement and exasperation.

'That redhead is awfully noisy,' she thought to herself, eyeing him with evident distaste.

She probably could have heard him all the way from the cave. She paused in her stride, and without really thinking, picked up a smooth stone from the ground and lobbed it at their flimsy half pitched tent. It ricocheted off one of the poles with a small metallic *ting* and hit the brown-haired boy smack in the chest. Despite that, it was the ginger one who let out a girlish, undignified squawk, which caused more birds to frantically scatter, releasing their own squawks of alarm, and him to whirl around to frantically scan the direction the rock had come from. The boy who had gotten hit put his head in his hands and shook it back and forth, as if he was so embarrassed for his friend that he couldn't even look at him. Kaitlyn ducked down with a hand sealed to her mouth, her shoulders quaking violently.

She peered through the gaps in the bush she was hiding behind and saw the redhead boy gesturing wildly and talking in nonsensical, stilted phrases.

She tilted her head, *'What an expressive person...'*

"Did you–what–is that a–where did–Wesley!?"

Kaitlyn clenched her jaw to keep her giggles silent, all the while her eyes were glowing with a dangerously mischievous light.

'This might actually be kind of fun.'

~~~~~~~~~~

"What the hell was that?" River asked Wes.

Well, at least he tried to. What actually came out of his mouth was a jumble of half sentences that even Wes wouldn't be able to decipher.

So instead, he just continued screeching and waving his arms around like an idiot.

Cause that's what he was good at–being an idiot.

After a few moments Wes must have gotten really irritated with River's blubbering because he snapped, "Could you be any louder? I don't think the people back home can hear you yet!"

"Who's going to hear us? The wild girl?" River responded, albeit more than a little hysterically while still frantically glancing around.
~~~~~~~~~~

Then he froze, realizing what he had just said.

'Oh,' he thought somberly, shoulders relaxing and head rolling back with a sigh that almost sounded melancholic.

When he met Wes's gaze again, the male had his lips pursed and his eyebrows slightly raised in something akin to mild incredulity. "Not like she might be lurking out there...*or anything*," Wes drawled sarcastically.

Looking appropriately sheepish, River scratched at his nape with a careful grin, "Oops..."

'Oops,' Wesley mimed before shaking his head. He did that a lot.

River glanced around, doing his best to keep his mind off the wild girl. They did come here to get away from everyday life too, a little break before the chaos of their senior year and college applications started.

They continued to set up the tent, and as he happened to catch sight of a particularly long strand of grass, something mischievous broke out in River's too blue eyes, an impish grin splitting his lips.

When Wes's back was turned, he nonchalantly leaned down and plucked the blade of grass. He tip-toed up behind Wes, and ever so slowly, inserted the tip of the plant into his ear.

Wes twitched so violently he sent both his elbows jabbing into River's flanks, causing him to double over with a grunt. As he righted himself, he saw Wes vigorously rubbing his ear against his shoulder. The dark-eyed male slowly turned around, face deadpan and tent pole held aloft in his hand.

River paled, but he could see Wes's lips twitching.

"I'll kill you," Wes said as he inclined his head, taking a looming step forward, the metal rod of deliverance swinging lazy circles in the air. It came off rather non-threatening, seeing as River knew Wes was fighting a smile.

River tilted his head with faux sweetness paired with a

sharp grin. "As if that would get rid of me. You know I'll just come back to haunt you."

Wes looked up at him, noticed how fond that smile was, and blew a breath out through his mouth. His lips quirked up almost involuntarily, his eyes holding a faint gleam of something that couldn't be easily put into words. "Yeah, you're annoyingly stubborn like that."

When River's shoulders visibly relaxed, Wes tacked on conversationally, "Doesn't mean I still can't slap you around a bit."

River's gaze snapped to Wes's when Wes smacked the tent pole down pointedly into his hand with a leering grin. River made a sound of alarm as he frantically crouched down to grab his own pole before he attempted to flee from his impending doom.

Wes gave chase, and while no killing blows were dealt in the ten-minute face off around the clearing, Wes did manage to whack River in the back of the knees in retaliation, which sent him crumpling face first into the grass with a yelp.

Disgruntled and appropriately KO'd, River glared through the blades of green obstructing his vision, ignoring the throbbing behind his knees. Eventually, River mustered up the energy to roll onto his back, propping himself up on his elbows as he spat the taste of earth out of his mouth. He shot a scathing look over at his friend, who was whistling inconspicuously as he was once again swinging the pole around in wide circles.

"Bro, what is up with you and my knees? At this rate I'm gonna need a walker before college!"

Wes paused, his lips frozen in an 'oh' and pole halting mid-upward arc, "Who said you were smart enough to go to college, dumbass?"

Bristling, River struggled to a sitting position with a scowl, "I'm smarter than Josh, and he's going," River retorted as he flung out a hand.

Wes shrugged, dropping the pole and sauntering toward River. "If it makes you feel any better, I'll make sure to get you some really cool colored tennis balls to go on the bottom of your walker," he offered with a sharp grin as he held out a hand to River.

Expression comically blank, River replied, "Oh yeah, that makes me feel *a lot* better. It'll also ruin my chances of making any other friends that are, I don't know, *not* abusive."

"You wouldn't be able to do that even without the walker," snarked Wes with a smirk as he pulled River up.

River blinked. Then rolled his eyes before he laughed good-naturedly, "You're such an ass."

Wes leaned in towards the blue-eyed male and uttered suggestively, "But I'm *your* ass."

River's face morphed into an expression caught halfway between horror and disgust. "If you *ever* say that again, I'm divorcing our friendship," he stated as he stabbed a finger at him.

"Alright, alright," Wes said, "let's go finish the tent before *someone* gets any more ideas or decides to have another prima donna meltdown," he blew a dark strand of hair out of his face as it fell over his matching eyes.

River shoved him.

Wes shoved back.

They both laughed as they wrestled their way back to the half-pitched tent.

All the while, River's mind couldn't help wandering back to where that pebble had come from and if it really had been the wild girl's doing.

He shivered, and he wasn't even cold.

CHAPTER ELEVEN
COVER BLOWN

Lurking.

Kaitlyn scoffed.

Honestly, lurking?

Please.

Kaitlyn Amor did not lurk...she stalked. Afterall, there was a *distinct* difference.

She whirled around to Midnight, unable to maintain her silent treatment against her any longer. "Can you believe them? Psh...lurking. As if I'd do something so-so...*ugh*!"

She stomped away into the forest, the underbrush rustling loudly as she went, on her way back to lur-*stalk!* around the clearing. It had been a few hours since the boys first arrived and she was still reeling from the information she'd received. Going on what she overheard earlier, she was forced to acknowledge that these two were the same boys she'd rescued from The Voice five years ago...the same boys she'd nonsensically revealed herself to. And apparently, they remembered her too, if what they'd both said possessed any merit. The fact just made her want them to leave even more. She didn't need any potential upset that could bring The Voice back. With them returning after nearly falling victim to The Voice in the past, who is to say their presence wouldn't cause It to return?

Whatever the case, it was something she couldn't-wouldn't-risk. She wasn't sure if she'd be able to cope with a Scratchy Voice relapse. So, she slunk back to the boys' campsite and perched herself in the thicket encircling the grassy clearing. She observed as the redhead, whom she assumed was the one called 'River,' lit a match and tossed it on a pile of kindling.

It took a few seconds, but before long the small pile of tinder was erupting into animated flames that cast the surrounding area in a warm glow.

The dark haired one, who Kaitlyn, without really meaning to, nick-named 'Freckle Face' but whose real name was apparently 'Wes,' short for Wesley, poked River with the marshmallow stick he'd retrieved for him. River forcefully grabbed the stick and turned away with a pointed sniff.

Kaitlyn felt a pang deep in her chest as she watched them interact with each other. It made her miss–No. She didn't miss anything. *She didn't miss anything.* Her heart was being dumb and needed to back off and let her head do the talking instead. It was the safer option, even if her mind screwed her over sometimes, at least it knew what was best for her more often than not. Her heart, however, was just a troublesome thing. No sense or rationale in its decision making. She didn't need it. *She didn't need it.*

"Should we look for her?"

Kaitlyn's head snapped up so suddenly she felt a crick pop in her neck. She hissed silently, groping furiously at her stinging nape. She hadn't gotten any creepy vibes from the boys since their arrival. They actually seemed pretty harmless. Well, besides the fact that *they knew she was there!* Holy crap, what if these guys were a ragtag team of crazy teenage ax murders?! What if they came here to *kill* her!?

'Oh my god, oh my god, oh my god,' replayed in her head on loop.

In hindsight, she realized that A. she hadn't seen them unpack any axes, and B. if they really wanted to kill her, they would have been scouring the forest by now. Even if they weren't positive of her existence, they would probably be more afraid of her than she was of them.

She became distracted from her train of thought when Freckle Face's dark eyes caught the light of the fire, briefly melting into pools of molten honey. He turned his head to look at the other boy and the effect was lost. She let out a silent breath she didn't even know she was holding. Why was her heart suddenly beating so fast?

'*Weird...*' she made a face at herself.

Wes shrugged. "I dunno. I know we came out here on the belief that she exists, but we don't actually know if she's still here," he stated.

He looked to have fallen deep into thought.

"I mean, it's worth a shot. I know you think so too, otherwise you wouldn't be here. It can't be a coincidence that we all dreamed about the same girl in the same place. And why was she there anyway? Why did we all have to abandon our camping trips so early? How was she even surviving out here? And where did that rock come from earlier?" River pointed out.

An impish little grin spread over Wes's face. "It could have been something else. Or maybe it *was* her. *You think she's watching us right now?*"

Kaitlyn distinctly felt like she'd been called out. She crossed her arms with a mute huff, entirely put out. The audacity of this guy. She slipped soundlessly from the bush she was crouching in as she distantly heard River complain to Freckle Face for 'making him feel freaked out now.' She released an inaudible snicker; he would be a lot more freaked out when he woke up in the morning. She circled the clearing for the next few hours, ensuring she kept herself hidden from potential view. She eventually grew bored and decided to scale a tree and hang out there. She nearly dozed off until the stark sound of a zipper closing startled her into full consciousness.

From what she'd managed to gather in her sleepy haze, they never mentioned her again after that first instance. She had the unmistakable impression that they believed she existed but were still a little skeptical of this belief due to lack of evidence. She wished they would just drop the whole thing and forget about her like the rest of the world did. She didn't want to be believed in...at least that's what she told herself.

'Why'd you step back into view all those years ago then?' came unbidden to her mind.

She chewed her lip, lost in thought. She didn't have an answer, feeling as if during that lapse in conscious judgement, she'd been driven by a purpose that wasn't her own.

'Doesn't matter,' she told herself. *'I just need to get them to leave. Then it'll be okay again.'*

What she failed to consider was that what she was doing, might make them more inclined to believe in her, rather than push them away.

When loud snores resounded from the tent a little while later, Kaitlyn dropped soundlessly from the tree and went to work. She couldn't wait to see their faces in the morning.

She blatantly ignored the voice in her head that told her she missed hearing the sound of another person's voice that wasn't her own. That her motive for even bothering with any of this was that maybe, deep down, she wanted those two boys to find her, to *see* her.

Because maybe she was tired of being alone all the time.

~~~~~~~~~~

Wes blinked, nonplussed.

Okay. Something was going on here. There was no way. There was absolutely no way that this many leaves fell during the night. Especially since they had only congregated on top and around their tent. The rest of the clearing was spotless, nary a leaf to be seen.

Wesley forced his way out of the tent, leaves spilling
~~~~~~~~~~

unceremoniously into the space and burying a still sleeping River's feet. The male gave a ridiculously loud snore and rolled over. Wes sighed. He had no idea how he was going to explain this to River in a way that wouldn't lead to further evacuation of local wildlife. Honestly, they had done nothing to deserve to be terrorized by River's comically obscene screeches and squawks. Wes shook his head fondly as he gazed at his still sleeping friend.

'I suppose it can't be helped,' he mused to himself, directing his attention to the leaves that may as well have been swallowing the tent.

He glanced around warily, attempting to process the scene. He felt slightly put out; this entire situation was just plain weird.

'Could it have been...?'

He shook his head, as if to dislodge a pesky fly. He knew he came out here to see if that girl was here, but the thought of her actually existing left an unpleasant taste in his mouth. His stomach twisted in knots at the mere idea of a small child being forced to live and grow up out here all by themself. Surely, the reason and cause behind the wild girl's existence couldn't have been a good one. So he forced himself to not think about how the leaves had even gotten in such a state in the first place. If he allowed his mind to wander, it would raise questions he didn't have any answers to. Which would only result in even more maddening questions.

Fighting to keep his mind blank, with only a scowl adorning his lips, he trudged forth with the cleanup.

'What a pain,' he griped to himself.

With great reluctance and a lot of grumbling, he started scooping up the dewy leaves and depositing them in a pile off to the side of the tent. Rather than allow his mind to plague him with possibilities he was unwilling to consider, he preoccupied his mind by admiring the forest around him as he completed the mindless task.

They really were in a beautiful place, with tall, looming trees that allowed the morning sun to filter through their lush canopy and dapple the ground in flecks of pale gold. The foliage was thick around the outskirts of the clearing, providing a sense of protection. The trees were draped with various greenery and flowers that were scattered by a delicate hand in the grassy center of the clearing. It had been a long time since Wes had witnessed so much vibrancy collected in one place. It was an enchanting slice of magic away from a world that didn't believe in such frivolous things, a world that often relied on the rigidity of logic and was incapable of seeing beyond its own horizon.

He was almost done removing the leaves from around the tent when he heard it.

A muffled thud followed by an 'oof.'

Wes tensed at the sound, his body strung so tight he thought he might snap if a breeze so much as fluttered his hair. Was it...?

There was no way.

He turned around.

Or maybe there was a....

Wes screamed.

CHAPTER TWELVE
THESE MEMORIES LEFT BEHIND

Kaitlyn failed to register what was happening until she landed flat on her butt smack dab in the middle of the clearing, with a very much awake Freckle Face standing less than ten feet away.

She was just quietly snickering to herself as she watched Freckle Face grumble his way through clearing the leaves when she heard a snap from behind her. She whipped around as a large, furry black mass collided with her front, effectively head-butting the wind out of her and sending her careening past the treeline where she landed on the ground with a thump.

And here she was, on the grass, completely baffled, gawking, as she watched Midnight slink off into the forest with a knowing gleam in her unnaturally blue eyes.

She was going to murder that wolf.

While she slept.

Kaitlyn was yanked back to reality when she heard a distinctly girlish scream sound from behind her.

Oh, right.

She was so startled that she gave an obscenely loud yelp, clambering to her feet and whirling around to face the origin of the high-pitched noise. She was vaguely aware of the cacophony of alarmed twittering and frantic rustling within the trees. She made a mental note to die later at the irony of it all.

She was met with an expression that most likely mirrored her own: utter disbelief, wide eyes and mouth held ajar.

In her stupor, she never heard the third shout of alarm

before there was wild movement from within the tent followed by a blur of red shooting out between the open flaps. She only glanced over with a panicked look in her eyes when a body fell face first into the leaves outside the tent with a faint crunch.

River. Of course it was. She almost wanted to laugh.

'Can this get any worse?' she thought strickenly.

She should have fled into the forest right then without a backward glance. But her feet wouldn't move. She was rooted to the spot whether she liked it or not.

'What a mess,' she internally groaned.

River lifted himself from the leaf covered ground enough for his face to be clearly seen.

He blew a raspberry before shaking his head. "Aw yuck. That does not taste good, no sir."

Then, as if nothing had happened, he raised his head and met Wes's startled expression with a clueless tilt of the head. "Why are we screaming?"

After a short pause, Freckle Face made a fervent hand gesture in Kaitlyn's general direction. Bemused, River slowly turned his head, and froze. He looked like a deer caught in the headlights. Kaitlyn was positive she didn't look much better.

When the tension in the air became so tangible it might as well have been a physical entity, she felt the distinctly childish urge to yell 'boo' or something of the like, to break the strained atmosphere. Just as the first syllable was about to touch her tongue, however, River squeaked as his hands blindly searched the ground. When he came in contact with a stick, he snatched it up, scrambled to his feet, and took cover behind Freckles while brandishing the pitiful excuse of a weapon at Kaitlyn.

"W-who the hell're you?!" he exclaimed shakily.

Kaitlyn's mouth spoke without her permission.

"Oh, don't play dumb. You know exactly who I am," she snarled.

She immediately slapped a hand over her mouth and darted her eyes off to the side in mortification. She wanted to throttle something, particularly herself. Why was this happening? She dared a glance back at the two boys and they both looked so comically flabbergasted that the hand over her mouth took on the new purpose of forcefully holding back her laughs. Though it wasn't long before any humor she had dissipated as she remembered that the two males weren't supposed to be here.

She dropped her hand, letting it fall limply to her side and setting her mouth in a firm line. She steeled herself, staring them down. She had nothing left to lose, so she might as well say what she'd wanted to from the very beginning.

"You both need to leave. Right now," she demanded fiercely, her tone leaving no room for argument.

"What? Why?" River asked as he reluctantly lowered his stick and stepped delicately out from behind Wes.

Losing the confident momentum of her harsh persona, she suddenly found a particular blade of grass to be exceptionally *fascinating*. "It's not safe–well–it *used* to not be safe. But you both being here might make it not safe again."

There was a pause.

"Does this have anything to do with us seeing you when we were younger?"

Kaitlyn's head jerked up. It was the other boy who had spoken for the first time since he'd seen her. As she scanned his face, she couldn't distinguish one emotion from another. He wore a completely cool and collected mask. She felt the compelling urge to slap it off his face.

Kaitlyn's eyes narrowed, her teeth bearing slightly. "So, you believe in me now, huh?"

River furrowed his brows, "Huh? We believed in you from the start, right Wes?" Gazing imploringly at his friend.

Wes shrugged, though something in his eyes turned sad.

"I was on the more skeptical end of it. I didn't want to believe you were real because of what that would have implicated, but I couldn't deny that there was some form of strange connection of events."

River frowned but said nothing.

Kaitlyn was just wondering what 'implicated' meant.

There was a long silence, the only sounds present being the soft twitters of the birds and the faint rustle of the wind in the trees.

"Gah! This is insane! It's so messed up!" River exclaimed as he buried his pale hands into the longer strands of his hair.

Kaitlyn gave him a flat look. "Yeah? Look who you're talking to."

River shot her a puzzled look.

'Confusion looks cute on him...wait what?' Kaitlyn internally gawked at her mind's bold statement.

Careful to keep her face blank and her voice even, she responded, "How do you think I ended up here all by myself?"

Understanding dawned in River's eyes, softening them significantly. A quick glance at Wes's empathetic expression in addition to his previous statements told Kaitlyn he'd already taken this into consideration.

She growled viciously, "Listen, there's no time for this. You shouldn't have come here. You both need to leave before *It* comes back or else we might all be in trouble. So go home. Forget about this place...and forget about me."

She spun on her heel, intending to march out of the clearing when a voice called out.

"Wait!"

Kaitlyn faltered in her steps, eventually pausing, but she didn't turn around. A few moments later both the boys were jogging up to her, stopping a few feet in front of her. She kept her eyes on their bare feet.

"Don't go. We have so many questions. Up until about a

week ago we thought you were just part of a dream we had when we were kids. A bunch of our friends even had the same dream. We know the significance of this place regarding that dream. But I don't think either of us expected for you to actually be here. I was convinced, but I had no idea what I would've done if I came face to face with you. It should be impossible that you're here at all, and we want to know why. You don't seem dangerous like some of our friends speculated, and maybe we can help you," River spoke quietly.

Kaitlyn could tell it was his voice because of the slightly raspy timber it had compared to Wes's smoother one.

She glared up at them through her lashes.

She rolled her eyes at River's puppy dog expression and Freckle Faces' inquiring head tilt and tiny smile. "If I answer your questions, will you leave?"

The two boys shared a glance. "We leave when the week's up. That's how long we planned on staying here originally," Wes said reasonably.

It was fair enough, so Kaitlyn shuffled backwards until she reached one of the logs the boys had set up around the fire pit and plonked down unceremoniously onto the rough wood. She noted to herself not to shift around too much so she didn't get butt splinters.

'No one likes butt splinters,' she thought gravely.

The boys followed suit, both looking mildly surprised as they sat down side by side on the log next to hers.

Kaitlyn made sure to angle her body away from them so she didn't have to meet their blatant staring.

For a few moments, there was nothing but awkward silence.

'This is so weird,' Kaitlyn stressed to herself.

Finally getting fed up with the lack of talking on the boys' end, she asked exasperatedly, "So what do you want to know then?"

She tried to ignore how loud and unsettled her voice

sounded to her own ears.

"...Would you mind starting from the beginning?" Freckle Face half-whispered.

It seemed apparent to Kaitlyn that if she refused, she wouldn't be pushed, at least not from him, and it was that very fact that ultimately made the decision for her.

She heaved a sigh, dreading the act of digging up all the things she put so much time and effort into burying. But she knew she'd feel begrudgingly guilty if she left them in the dark. They didn't seem like bad people, not that she could really speak intelligently on the matter. But she had saved them once upon a time. While they had been strangers, they still saw her on that night so long ago, so she resolved herself to give them the truth, not because they asked, but because they deserved answers.

Spine rigid, she rotated her body toward them while keeping her eyes fixed on the surrounding nature. She took a deep breath and started from the beginning.

She told them about how she woke up alone in the forest, its looped state, The Voice, her struggle, she scars and the shadows, how she almost died and let The Voice win, the wolves, her determination to get back to her family, what The Voice had really done to them. She told them about the cave and the waterfall and how she managed to keep surviving after her initial close call with the unforgiving cold, about the ruts she'd fallen into, about her growth. She told them how she saved all those kids and how she hadn't meant to reveal herself five years ago. She told them about the passing of the seasons and how she adapted. She told them about The Voice weakening, the circumstances in which she realized the forest was unlooped. She told them how there were kids before her, why she stayed and even rationalized her thought process to them so they would understand. She told them everything as the sun rose higher and higher into the sky. Everything she could drag up from the depths of her mind about what she'd gone though, all the ding-dong ditches at death's door, about her sparse moments of joy, and finally her peaceful acceptance up until the moment she was, without a shred of elegance, forced in front of their faces.

And through it all they both uttered not a word. They just sat and listened to her ramble as she refused to meet their eyes. When she grew quiet, her chest felt tight and the backs of her eyes stung. Her hands clenched into fists. She felt her chipped nails dig into the calloused flesh of her palms. Her jaw tightening painfully as she squeezed her eyes shut. She had to fight back the emotions raging inside her, the dam that so desperately wanted to burst. With the retelling of her story, a monstrous hurricane had been unleashed in her head, a spitting wildfire in her heart, and a gaping pit where her soul should have been. She'd forced it to be locked away for so long that it had festered in the abyss of Pandora's box. Now it was wide open, and there was no going back. The past she'd mercilessly repressed was in the present now, and it wouldn't be returning to its box without a fight.

She wasn't sure she had it in her to fight anymore. She wasn't sure she even wanted to.

A hesitant hand was laid carefully on her bare, sun-tarnished shoulder.

A single tear rolled down her cheek, flaring gold in the fading sunlight as it rolled off her chin.

Another crack formed inside her.

CHAPTER THIRTEEN
FRIENDS WITH THE WILD GIRL?

River watched as Wes laid a hand on the girl's tan shoulder. His heart ached from everything she'd recounted to them, and he was struggling to not just tackle the girl into one of his infamous hugs. But he barely knew her, and from the way she just furiously wiped at her face and flinched away from Wes's hand, River's sentiment wouldn't have been very appreciated. He felt like an ass for making her cry, even if it was unintentional. He couldn't even begin to know where to go from here, but he knew he believed her. She had no reason to lie to them and if she had wanted to harm them, she would have done so already, considering it's likely she'd known they were here since they arrived. Maybe he was being naive, as his friends never failed to remind him.

And yeah, sometimes he really could be naive, so his friends were right. He trusted too easily and yadda... yadda... yadda... tell him something he didn't know. Despite being aware of this, he was willingly going to give this girl, who was practically a stranger, the benefit of the doubt. He believed her. He *did*, even if what she told them sounded like the ravings of a lunatic. It was just so difficult to wrap his head around, how she was erased from her parents' lives, just like that. River recalled that the exact word she had used was 'disappear,' and with that thought, he was suddenly drawn back to something his father had said when he was younger.

River and Wes had been playing hide and seek at River's house, the former seeking the latter for a good half an hour before stomping into the sunlit kitchen. Of which where his father, with his own red hair catching fire in the late morning sun, stood leaning against the counter as he nursed a cup of coffee.

"Daaadd!" The young boy had whined with his arms crossed petulantly.

Looking over at him, his dad merely quirked an eyebrow in acknowledgment.

"Dad!" the boy repeated.

His father set his mug down on the counter with a soft thud. "What is it Rivera?" he asked with an amused glint in his blue eyes.

River scrunched his face up, looking like he'd just caught a whiff of a particularly foul odor. "Don't call me that."

"But it's your name."

"No, my name's River!"

His father smiled a knowing smile, showing off dazzling white teeth. "Alright, alright. River, what is it?"

Abruptly the small boy flung his arms out dramatically, looking entirely fed up with everything. "I can't find Wes; I've looked everywhere! He's just disappeared!"

River's father pushed off the counter with a chuckle and moved to crouch in front of his pouting son.

With a fond smile, the adult said, "People don't just disappear, son. He's got to be somewhere, you might just have to look a little harder, that's all."

With a ruffle of his son's hair, the older male stood up and ushered a newly determined River back into his search.

'People don't just disappear, huh?' River mused wryly to himself.

"Stop brooding."

River's head immediately snapped up to find Wes simpering at him and the girl avoiding his gaze with both lips sucked into her mouth.

"I wasn't brooding! I was...thinking. You should try it sometime, Wes."

Wes looked wholly offended, a look River lived for. But before the freckled boy could retort anything back, the girl stood, dusted off her... (Was that a deer skin?) dress and glanced up at the sky. "I need to leave now. Don't follow me."

She started to turn, but she froze when River spoke up.

"What's your name?"

At first, River thought she wasn't going to answer, but was pleasantly surprised when she offered, albeit a bit reluctantly, "...Kaitlyn."

River smiled, "I'm River," he jerked his thumb to the male beside him, "and that idiot is Wes."

Kaitlyn nodded shortly and began walking away again. Feeling slightly panicked at not knowing if they would see her again, he rushed forward just as she was about to enter the treeline. "Will you come back tomorrow?"

She glanced sharply over her shoulder at him.

He reared up abruptly, barely stifling an embarrassing squeak.

The harsh lines of her face suddenly softened slightly. She replied in such a quiet voice that River had to strain his ears to hear her, "Maybe."

Then she was gone.

Perhaps people could disappear after all.

~~~~~~~~~~

Kaitlyn honestly had no idea what she was doing. No idea why she was walking back through the forest toward the grassy clearing with a tent containing two very peculiar boys. And having no idea why she was even bothering when they would be gone soon anyway, even more so the fact why she seemed to care so much that they would be.

She tipped her head back to gaze at the patches of pale blue sky peeking through the thick canopy. She sighed.

"You've really done it this time," she said to no one in particular.
~~~~~~~~~~

She continued walking until dirt transitioned to grass, taking a seat on the same log she had the day prior, and waited.

She didn't have to wait long, for only a short while later, the dark-haired boy was emerging from the tent whilst simultaneously rubbing the sleep from his eyes. Kaitlyn watched with mild amusement as the boy jumped once he gained enough awareness to realize she was there.

She watched him watch her. "You're not going to scream again, are you?"

He scoffed, but Kaitlyn could see mirth dancing in his eyes. He eventually made his way over to the logs and sat down across from her. "I'm assuming you were the one who half buried our tent in leaves yesterday morning?"

Kaitlyn rolled her eyes. "Who else?"

Wes shrugged. "Kinda thought it was something else."

Kaitlyn couldn't tell if he was being sarcastic or not.

She raised an eyebrow, one side of her mouth quirking up in a leer. "Yeah? Kinda like you thought something else threw a rock at you?"

"Of course you were listening. Was there anything you didn't hear, you creeper?" She noticed there was a playful lilt to his voice.

She scrunched her nose up at the term 'creeper.' "You're in my territory. I have a right to 'creep.'"

Leaning back on his hands, Wes replied with an overly cheerful, "Fair enough."

There was a lull in the pair's small conversation and Kaitlyn found herself racking her brain for something to say.

Eventually, she said, "You seem to be taking this well."

He tilted his head to the side. "Taking what well?"

He looked like a puppy, or rather, like one of the wolves and she got the sudden urge to ruffle his unruly hair. Her fingers twitched and she clenched them in as tight a fist as she could, shoving the ridiculous thought away.

She made a flippant hand gesture at herself and the clearing around them. "Oh you know, me, the entire situation, *the fact that there's a pack of wild wolves literally a screaming distance away.*"

Wes shrugged. "I'm trying not to think too hard about it. It's easier and less stressful to go with the flow and take things as they come. And it's not like we had no idea you existed, we just thought you were some weird dream or hallucination we all had as kids. We touched on the fact that you might've been real, but obviously, we were still skeptical."

Little did Kaitlyn know that Wes had actually thought *very* hard on it. To the point where it took him hours to fall asleep the night prior because he'd only been able to stare at the ceiling of the tent in a daze. He'd been unable to do anything *but* think.

After a long pause of Kaitlyn just staring blankly at Wes, he added on with an amused huff, "If it makes you feel any better, River freaked out for a solid ten minutes after you left."

Her lips quivered. "Why am I not surprised?"

A sneeze sounded behind her. "Are you guys talking about me?"

Both Kaitlyn and Wes whipped around to see River poking his head out of the tent opening, eyes narrowed in the muted sunlight that streamed into his face. Kaitlyn fought the urge to snort.

After screwing up his face some more until his eyes adjusted to the daylight, he shuffled barefoot out of the tent and made his way over to sit down by Wes. He yawned loudly.

"You came back..." River spoke quietly as he picked at a stray thread on his plaid pajama pants.

Kaitlyn raised an eyebrow. "Not a lot gets passed you, does it?"

Wes tried to muffle a guffaw but was wholly unsuccessful as he soon received a punch in the shoulder.

"I swear, first you and now Kaitlyn! I can't catch a break. And you should brush your hair, Wes. That bird up there looks to be eyeing your nest."

Wes immediately brought his hands up to shield his head in what appeared to be a knee-jerk reaction as he glanced feverishly around the trees. Upon seeing there were no birds in sight and realizing the absurdity of such an occurrence, he scowled at his now smug friend.

"Not so fun being on the butt end of a joke, is it?" River poked Wes's ribs repeatedly.

Kaitlyn had little time to ponder the fact that they both seemed to have become comfortable with her presence surprisingly quickly, because in the amount of time it took for her to blink, Wes had launched himself at River and sent them both crashing to the ground. She watched with wide eyes as they started wrestling with each other. It distinctly reminded her of the way she and her sister used to rough house, of the way she herself would wrestle with the wolves. And as she watched the two males roll around on the ground with smiles on their faces, their laughter filling the air, tears welling unbidden in her bright eyes, she was struck with how much of her childhood she had missed.

How many years of human companionship and laughter and fun that had been stolen from her, stripped away and shredded before she even knew what hit her. Sure, she'd had some of that with the wolves, with Midnight, but it wouldn't have been the same, would it? You can't replace family; she remembered reading in a book once. It felt like a veil had been lifted and a sack of rocks had been tied around her neck. So much, so much she had missed out on in her life. So many birthdays, so many Christmases and pivotal life moments that one built beautiful houses of memories on. And it was all because of The Voice. All *Its* fault. She felt the pure hatred she harbored for the entity flare back to life for a brief, enraged moment, before it flickered and died like a weak flame. All that remained was a hollow space where the love of her family should have been, the memories. The emotions were swirling around within her, ricocheting off the inside of her skin, but she felt none of them, only knew that they were there, waiting for the right moment to sink their teeth in and never let go.

She dug her chipped nails into the palm of her hand until she felt the soft flesh give way to blood. Watching it trail down her hand and interweave itself into the grooves of the wood she was sitting on grounded her, and she felt like she could breathe again. She blinked the tears away and stood up. Her sudden movement must have caught the boys' attention because their tussle in the grass came to a halt, Wes having River in a loose choke hold and River ruthlessly clawing at Wes's freckled forearms with both of his hands. They stared at her owlishly, and any other time, Kaitlyn might have openly laughed at them.

Instead, she attempted to put some life into her voice before she asked, "Do you want to see the other clearing I told you about yesterday?"

They were both still for a moment, then River's eyes lit up and he stumbled to his feet, Wes following at a more leisurely pace. While the two of them seemed to be equally interested, Kaitlyn noticed that there was still apprehension in their eyes. To quell any worry, she tacked on, "The wolves won't hurt you...I promise."

They must have seen some measure of sincerity in her eyes, because they gave twin nods with only a hint of uncertainty plaguing their features.

"Lead the way!" River exclaimed boisterously.

Kaitlyn quickly turned to the direction she planned on taking them in to hide the smile that brightened her face. The red head's energy was annoyingly infectious, but she found herself not minding it too much. Even as she felt like she was coming apart at the seams, it was hard to notice when she was surrounded by River's positive energy. While the presence of the two males had originally dug up painful days, after witnessing their friendship, she admitted to herself that it was...nice, having them around with sounds of their bickering filling the air. It made her feel somewhat normal again, and although she knew it wouldn't last, she decided she would enjoy it while she could. Even if it meant there was no turning back, even if it would eventually destroy her.

'You could always leave with them~' a distant, lilting voice rose from the depths of her mind, dangling the notion tantalizingly in front of her nose.

She slapped it away without a second thought. There was no way. Her place was here, in the forest, ensuring The Voice didn't return. If she left with them, who knows what would happen. On top of that, she would be returning to a world completely different from the one she entered from. She wouldn't put herself through that sort of turmoil and stress. She would have nowhere to go, a shard of glass among the smooth, delicate flower petals of society. It would be like trying to fit a square peg in a round hole. She didn't belong to their world anymore, hadn't for a long time, and while there was a tint of bitterness to the thought, she still had no desire to ever return to that world.

Pushing everything to the back burner, she continued to lead the boys to the cave, readily answering any questions they popped off at her. Kaitlyn noticed they were making an effort to keep the questions lighthearted and didn't let them stray too far into anything pertaining to her life before the forest. The gesture did not go unappreciated; her wounds had endured enough salt for the time being.

After a slew of River's cursing directed at the large tree root he had stubbed his now sneaker clad toe on, Kaitlyn was shouldering aside a group of branches and stepping into the place she had come to consider home. As soon as she heard two pairs of footsteps stop behind her, she turned around to face the owners of those footsteps. She wasn't surprised to find matching looks of awe on their faces, seeing as she had reacted in much the same way her first time seeing it. With a smug little smile pulling at her lips, she stepped off to the side with a wide, grand sweep of her arm and proclaimed, "Welcome to paradise."

<div align="center">~~~~~~~~~</div>

When Kaitlyn assured the boys that they were safe by showing them the sleeping wolves harmlessly tucked away in the back of the cave, they both enthusiastically started venturing around the clearing. She would wait and see if they found the secret entrance to the waterfall first before she made any effort to show them directly. She didn't bother muffling her snicker at the thought of one of them stumbling into it the way she had so many years before.

She sighed. *'Years, huh?'*

It really had been years, and she suddenly felt them all catching up with her as she watched the boys explore her home with eyes alight with wonder. It was a strange sensation, experiencing all her memories of this place play like a slide show through her mind. She closed her eyes, faintly aware of laughter in the distance. When was the last time she'd heard another's laughter, seen another's smile, heard another voice that wasn't her own? She let herself bask in the faraway sounds of their voices, found herself not minding them moving about her personal haven as they pleased. She was grateful for their presence despite initially loathing it. So long as she was here, The Voice wouldn't come back, she was certain of that now and no longer felt the need to usher the two teenagers out of the forest.

Their appearance had shaken her, continued to do so if she was being honest, but she was willing to bear the pain

175

if it meant having human company again. The wolves were nice and all, but they weren't the same. She felt a twinge of guilt at the thought, without the wolves she wouldn't be here. She owed them her life and then some. They had taken her in as their own, no hesitation. They'd kept her warm when the wind blew ice and the nights grew cold, comforted her when the emotional agony escaped through her eyes and dampened the dirt at her feet. They'd supported her when she couldn't find it in herself to stand on her own. And they never left. They were always there when everyone else had gone, and Kaitlyn made sure to never forget that again.

Something poked her arm.

She pried her eyes open and was met with the tan face of Wes staring at her with both eyebrows raised.

She squinted at him. "What?"

<div align="center">~~~~~~~~~</div>

This place was crazy gorgeous. He'd never seen something so ethereal in his life and all he wanted to do was draw it or paint it or *something*, but he knew that nothing he did would ever do it any justice. So he settled for taking picture after picture, at least this way he could capture its beauty in time while simultaneously being able to look back on it whenever he wanted.

River was doing the same thing, he noticed. He promptly rolled his eyes when he examined further though. His klutz-of-a-friend had fallen into the lake, drenching his entire right side and leaving Wes moderately impressed that the redhead had managed to keep his phone mostly out of the sparkling water's clutches.

In response to Wes's bewildered look, River had only declared, "'Twas an honor to be touched by these magnificent waters!"

Wes had wondered if his supposed "dramatics" had begun to rub off on River. Not that the notion was all that jaw-dropping.

Once Wes took as many pictures as his little artistic heart desired, (River's words, not his), he turned his attention back to the cave where the wolves were sleeping. It was a black stain against the vibrant green, and although it looked slightly ominous, he found himself drawn there. Gradually making his way over, still soaking in the scenery, he tentatively stuck his head in the entrance. The space was vast, his eyes widening in pleasant surprise upon catching the faint scent of honeysuckle. He would have expected the place to be dank or musty and smell like dog, but evidently, that wasn't the case.

'Kaitlyn's touch, probably,' he reasoned to himself.

Deeming it safe, he moved a little further in so he could get a better look. It was almost like a tunnel, one that curved modestly to the right with a high ceiling and a broad passage. Wes was nearly six feet tall and in turn, had a wide wingspan. But even as he stuck out his arms, there was still a few feet between his hands and the wall on either side. The wolves, he noticed with slight apprehension, were bathed in shadow at the very back of the cave, snoozing away. There was a rolled up sleeping bag not too far from the canines and a few animal pelts nailed to the walls. The dirt floor was also covered in fresh smelling fir needles. Cushion, Wes suspected. There were also various white patterns on the parts of the wall not adorned with furs. As he peered closer, his mouth parted slightly as he realized they were intricately carved into the rock. He wasn't sure what the carvings were meant to depict, only that they added a tasteful charm to the place. He was running his fingers reverently over the grooves in the stone when he froze.

'Wait. I'm being weird, aren't I? This is her bedroom. *Where she* sleeps.'

Wes hastily backed out of the cave, realizing how nosy he was being. He internally reprimanded himself for invading her personal space, even if it wasn't all that private since anyone could literally walk right in. It was then that he spotted the girl in question a few yards away, leaning against a tree with her arms crossed and her eyes closed.

She gave no indication that she heard him approach, and after a few minutes of her remaining unresponsive (was she asleep?), he poked her in the arm, observing that she had a smattering of freckles under her cheeks and across her nose.

'Kinda cu—' he cut himself off, *'Nope, nope. Not going there.'*

Before he could dwell on it for too long, her eyes were squinting up at him.

'Wow she's really short.

"What," she slurred.

Wes barely registered what she said because he was too busy reeling from the color of her eyes. He hadn't gotten a good look until now, but they weren't a typical blue like he'd originally thought. There were various tones of green and turquoise, hints of amber intermixed with gold flecks centered around the iris. Was it weird that he kind of wanted to dive into them and listen to all the stories they were willing to tell? Until now, he'd refrained from thinking too hard about her situation, at least if he could help it. She clearly didn't want to talk about it more than she had to, and he'd already received the answers to his questions. The only thing he could do after that was try to brush it from his mind, absorb her story and then lock it away.

But now? He didn't want to keep trying to deny it, to inhibit his own thoughts and insights, about how scared she must have been and just how wrong what happened to her was. How was she even standing, this girl with eyes who put sunsets to shame? He and River had briefly discussed their options last night, how they could help her, even if she was a mere stranger. They'd both agreed that there wasn't much of anything they *could* do, other than offer for her to come back with them. But that came with its own set of issues.

He looked at her, really looked at her for the first time; she was all sharp angles, unkempt auburn hair and unevenly pigmented skin dotted with countless freckles and sunspots. Her eyes glinted with a savage light that the current society would've found disconcerting. Her overall appearance just screamed...wild, untamed. To the modern world, she wasn't what one would consider traditionally beautiful, but that was okay, she didn't need to be. None of us do.

Wes, for the first time in his life, was at a complete loss, not only at what to do, but also because he could not look away from those damn eyes no matter how hard he tried.

'Why'd I come over here again?'

In that moment he was snapped from his reverie when River came bounding over, tripped over his untied laces, and just missed taking Wes to the ground with him.

Ignoring River, Wes turned back to Kaitlyn, his hand coming up to scratch at his nape. She was looking at both of them like she wasn't sure whether she wanted to laugh or walk away.

"So, you've acclimated yourself to this place pretty well."

She squinted at him again, retorting, "Akka-what? What's that mean?"

By this point River had re-tied his shoes and righted himself to join Wes in gawking at the girl. But then again, it actually made sense why she didn't know the meaning of the word, seeing as she only had the vocabulary of, from what Wes could tell, an elementary kid.

'And the sarcasm of a snarky teenager,' his mind supplied unwarranted.

Wes shared a look with his friend, watching out of the corner of his eye as the auburn haired girl's eyes progressively narrowed in suspicion.

'Oh, this could be fun.'

After Wes patiently explained the definition of 'acclimate,' he asked Kaitlyn about the markings on the cave wall. According to her, there was no rhyme or reason to them. All she'd done was use a blade she'd found to carve them whenever she needed to rest her mind for a bit. When asked if he could take a photograph, she gave him permission to take one photo. *One.* How could she be so cruel?

After he was done internally fawning over her unintentional artwork, he noticed an impish gleam in her unearthly eyes. He couldn't decide whether he liked it or not.

"You guys wanna see something cool?" she asked with the closest thing to a smile Wes had seen on her thus far.

They both agreed, Wes a bit skeptical but overall giving in to his curiosity. River was practically vibrating with excitement as she led them toward the waterfall.

The vision that awaited them was without a doubt the best part of the whole place.

<div style="text-align:center">~~~~~~~~~~</div>

Kaitlyn watched with wicked glee as Wes and River fell noisily through the stone and into the small cavern behind the waterfall. She heard two wet smacks followed by a squawk and a long chain of very creative curse words that had Kaitlyn cackling so animatedly that she nearly fell over. She eventually managed to stagger through the rock as well, still giggling hysterically. She really did fall over though when she was met with twin disgruntled looks connected to disheveled appearances.

While she was so overtaken with laughter, she wasn't privy to the way both the boys' faces broke out into their own grins. Perhaps they were just glad to see the girl who hadn't even cracked a smile, let alone laugh, since they'd encountered her, do both of those things.

They regarded each other for a moment, then turned their attention back to the girl smiling brightly up at them before glancing fleetingly back at each other. A look passed between them, an unspoken thought but still mutually understood.

'We did that,' it said.

~~~~~~~~~~

The three teenagers spent the rest of the day goofing around in the cavern. It eventually fell way into a heated water battle once Kaitlyn had sent the guys toppling through the waterfall, but not before River had snagged her wrist at the last second, taking her with them as they plummeted the short distance to the sparkling water below.

She didn't think she'd ever had that much fun in her life. Or if she had, she certainly couldn't remember.

When the sun began its sluggish descent in the sky, the trio sunned themselves on the waterfall's rocky clifftop. They elaborated why they had come here camping in the first place and Kaitlyn asked them about their life back in what she learned to be Hillsboro; she realized with a start that it wasn't all that far from her own hometown. She ignored the way the thought made her chest hurt momentarily. They happily answered any questions she had, and in response, she opened the table for them to ask anything they wanted about her life before she was abandoned.

She wouldn't lie, could not stand to do such a thing to herself anymore; it hurt. It hurt a lot. Each name she spoke that she hadn't even let herself *think* of in years was acid on her tongue. Each detail she wrangled from her
~~~~~~~~~~

stubborn mind felt like ripping a layer of skin off every time she managed to haul one to the surface. Each word that left her lips was heavy with agony, the retelling of a life that no longer belonged to her, but rather a person whom she no longer recognized. A distant past that she didn't comprehend just how desperately she was clinging to until she'd recalled it in as much detail as she could bare. It was torture in its most gentle form, and while it made her heart ache in ways she hadn't experienced since she first found out the fate of her family, there was something freeing about it. Like she could finally lay it all to rest rather than lock it back up. There were still storms raging in her head, still mayhem terrorizing her soul, her emotions still in a ferocious uproar. But the entirety of the chaos rampaging inside her that had devastatingly escaped her control had become something horrifically beautiful. From the cracks sprung blooming wildflowers, bestowing the gift of life from the torrential rains.

She looked off to the side at a patch of greenery sprouting in between two rocks. Caught within the vermillion rays of the dying sun, was a plant with three thin stems dotted with tiny leaves, each tipped with a dainty baby blue flower.

Tears gathered in her eyes, the world around her blurring into a brilliant kaleidoscope of blazing reds and oranges and golds. She turned back to look at the two boys sitting beside her, not expecting for their eyes to be on her as well.

It was there they sat, watching Kaitlyn watch them. River's red hair was set ablaze in the embers of the fading light, his blue eyes caressed by colors of an ocean. Wes's eyes glistened like old copper pennies, his hair holding a matching sheen amidst the fountain of waves. His kind face was littered with dozens of freckles that traveled down his neck. They reminded Kaitlyn of the sprinkle of cinnamon she would always request over her hot chocolate when she was younger.

They both tilted their heads at her simultaneously, making Kaitlyn wonder whether it was a planned action. Then they both jabbed her in the arm with a playful light in their eyes.

And she finally knew how to find her own hope again.

She just couldn't remember it ever being this terrifying.

~~~~~~~~~

Throughout the following days, it became routine for the boys to purposefully use large and complicated words they knew Kaitlyn wouldn't understand. It was so easy to get her worked up that River and Wes just couldn't resist. Though they still took the time to explain all of the meanings afterward. Kaitlyn was torn between begrudging gratitude and wanting to thoroughly acquaint them with her right foot. The former won out...mostly.

Kaitlyn also officially introduced River and Wes to her pack. In her opinion, it went surprisingly well. No tails were stepped on and all limbs remained intact and bite free. Although the boys were more than a little on edge and the wolves were slightly hesitant in their direct approach, by the end of the meeting River had been tackled and nearly licked to death by Midnight's pups and Wes was engaged in a very whimsical conversation (complete with a full set of theatrical hand gestures), with the massive dark wolf herself.

Kaitlyn found the whole ordeal immensely entertaining. She would be keeping the memory of Wes and Midnight's interaction safety tucked away, the way Midnight had woofed in response to one of Wes's rhetorical questions, followed by the freckled teenager exclaiming with his hands thrown wide, "Exactly! Finally, someone gets it!"

River had asked Wes if he had finally gone senile. Kaitlyn had merely snorted a laugh as the bickering she
~~~~~~~~~

had come to associate with the two roared to life.

One evening, the boys let Kaitlyn explore their phones, seeing as she never had the chance to have one of her own. She particularly enjoyed the music feature; River and Wes had roared with laughter so hard they'd nearly fallen off their logs upon witnessing Kaitlyn's horrified expression when she stumbled upon "I Like Big Butts" from one of Wes's and River's shared playlists. After that, she decided she hadn't missed much when it came to electronics and left it at that. She did, however, allow herself to be convinced with minimal protest to dance goofily around the firelit clearing with the boys to some catchy pop songs. That was a fun night.

Kaitlyn took the time to teach the boys everything she knew about the forest and surviving there, as per their eager request. To say it had been a hassle would have been an understatement. Between Wes pointing and asking "What's this?" at every little thing without giving her any time to answer before gesturing to something else, and River wanting to eat any plant that so much as *existed* in his presence, she'd been ready to tear out her own hair. She was certain they were doing it on purpose. There was no way either of them was that clueless. But, although annoying, she probably laughed more on that day alone than she had in her entire life. Hours filled with frustrating hilarity that left the best of aches lingering in her sides until the next morning. She would have shown them how to hunt, but the idea of killing and skinning an animal in front of them left a particularly uneasy feeling in her gut. From what she could deduce, neither of them had ever been hunting before, and she didn't want to subject them to the final cry of an animal's death. It still bothered her at times, left her eyes damp as the high-pitched noise permeated the air, and she'd been hearing it for years.

Somewhere along the way, their tentative, unsure start gave way to a friendship that grew far deeper than what should have been possible within a mere few days. None of them could really pinpoint an exact moment where the subtle shift occurred, but it mattered little in the grand scheme of things. Time held little authority in that forest, not for those days they were together, at least. They were in their own little dazzling bubble of paradise.

But time was running out.

CHAPTER FOURTEEN
STORM

It was the second to the last night the boys were scheduled to leave, that they finally addressed the elephant that had been lurking in the back of their minds in recent days despite the carefree nature they exuded.

Kaitlyn sat hunched over with her arms resting on her bare knees as she gazed into the fire, the sharp angles of her face cast in deep, writhing shadow. Her eyes were unfocused on the twirling flames as they weaved a spell of smoke and dying ember.

The dark sky overhead was overcast, the air thick and heavy, the intensity of the wind steadily increasing and harboring a faint chill. She inhaled a silent breath through her mouth, tasted the dampness of oncoming rain on her tongue.

The breeze interwove its fingers through her short hair, making it dance in tandem with the fire that crackled before her.

Without taking her eyes from the blaze in front of her, she spoke to the two males off to her immediate left.

"It'll rain soon," she spoke absentmindedly, softly, so as not to shatter the fragile illusion of peace that concealed the solemn atmosphere that had befallen over the three of them.

One of the boys, Wes, Kaitlyn suspected, made a noncommittal sound in the back of his throat. She was positive that if she looked over, she would see the freckled male's hair being similarly handled by the air currents. A corner of her mouth twitched.

It was silent after that. For how long, she couldn't tell. The concept of time had abandoned her long ago. For some time, they all sat there, the wind howling through the trees, the leaves rustling loudly and the branches moaning with ominous creaks. It seemed as if the land around them was waiting for something, thrumming with a strange energy Kaitlyn had never experienced before. The atmosphere felt perilous and unsteady, like one wrong move would upset the precarious balance and send them all tumbling off the precipice they were all teetering on.

She hunched further in on herself.

She wasn't surprised when River's gentle timber broke the peace.

"You could come back with us."

His voice held a flimsy undertone of hope, as if he already knew it would be crushed, but couldn't help himself regardless.

Kaitlyn's toes curled into the grass.

Her blunt, chipped nails dug into the flesh right above her elbow.

When she spoke next, it was with a forced casualness that she was all too aware wasn't fooling anyone. She felt like a live wire, like her skin was stretched too tight over her bones. Her whole form tense, and it was only a matter of time before something had to give.

"Say I did come with you. Then what?"

A pause.

She heard a gulp.

She patiently listened as River rambled on about what would happen if she returned to Hillsboro with them. How one of their parents would be happy to take her in, how she could meet their friends, and could be homeschooled until she caught up to the level of education she was supposed to be at. That maybe even one day, she could return to Forest Grove and see–.

She didn't let him finish, *couldn't* let him. Couldn't

continue to listen to that foolish sliver of hope in his voice.

"No," she interrupted, voice hard as tempered steel.

She could imagine River's flinch.

A tense moment passed.

She sagged into herself, her head falling into her hands.

She repeated in a broken whisper, "No."

There was something about the pose that was so desperately hopeless that the boys were at a loss for words. Tears came unbidden to Wes's eyes and he had to clench his jaw to keep them from falling. His heart ached.

The tree branches above were thrashing violently with the screaming wind, and it very well may have been a physical embodiment of the storm in Kaitlyn's head.

"I can't go back with you and you know it," her voice was ragged and choked with turbulence squirming beneath the surface of her skin. "It wouldn't work. Too many problems."

For the first time that night, she looked up at them, silent tears dampening her face, making her eyes appear brighter than normal. "I'm not something that needs tamed. I've been here for almost eight years; I knew what I was doing when I decided to stay. Maybe I could go back, but they would try to cage me, and I won't let them. I like my life here more than I think I would like a new life out there. In case you forgot, in the world you both come from, I don't exist. And there's nothing you can do to change that."

If she were being honest, she almost hated the two people sitting in front of her. Before they arrived, she'd been under the impression that she'd made peace with her life before the forest and accepted that she would never see her family again. She thought she'd begun to heal, that the outside world no longer held meaning to her. But then these two waltzed in and messed everything up! They made her remember things she didn't want to, bringing everything roaring back to the forefront of her mind. It became apparent she hadn't healed at all, just tricked herself into believing she had. She'd sculpted perfect walls around herself, and they came bursting in with rocks spewing from their laughter, smashing her foundation with their smiles, as if those walls were made from the thinnest of glass. It was all their fault that she was left fumbling for something to keep herself steady.

It wasn't fair! Why'd they have to come here?! Why'd Midnight have to go and push her into that clearing, all but forcing her to make contact? These boys had turned her world upside down, given her some of the best moments of her life. They'd nudged her in the direction of the strength she needed to restore the hope she hadn't even realized she'd lost, throttled the fragile world she established for herself, and for what? Just so they could leave in two days, leave her here all alone just like her parents, with a sinking feeling in her stomach because she was second guessing her decision to remain in the forest? Realizing that even if she did regret it, it was already too late to make it better? That she would have to live the rest of her life wondering, 'what if?'

The unknown had never bothered her before, but they made her see all the flaws in her plan, all the unfinished ends she thought she'd stitched up. It was utter torture to come to the revelation that things could have been different, if only she'd made a different choice.

There was a booming crack and the heavens unleashed upon them. Thunder shook the ground and lightning splintered across the sky. The rain came down in buckets, soaking them instantly.

A wolf howled in the distance, the eerie sound practically muted by the raging storm; she felt the urge to echo it. Instead, she slid limply from the log onto the ground, her face open to the merciless sky, letting the heavy drops mix with the salty ones on her face. It felt like she was splitting apart like the lightning split the sky, the thunder in her head echoed continuously above...but drenched in the torrential rain, she was shocked to find that it felt like being reborn. Her anger and sorrow ebbed away with the water flowing down her body. She felt nothing, and it was glorious. There was no more voice in her head relentlessly shouting at her, no more all-consuming emotion that threatened to suffocate her, no more anything. She was a blank slate, washed clean with the physical embodiment of the tempest inside her that had escaped through her pores. There was no more chaos within the caverns of her soul, the receptacle of her heart or the winding tunnels of her mind.

It became clear to her that something inside her was very much astray, probably had been from the start. Suddenly there were two other bodies kneeling in front of her, clothes and hair plastered down to their skin. She tilted her head to gaze at them through the pouring rain. They had taken her on a nearly unbearable rollercoaster over the past few days, leaving within her with a paradox of a soaring spirit and a bitter heart. The feelings she'd expressed in her whirlwind of an inner uproar only moments ago had come and gone. She harbored none of it towards them, not really. Her brain had just needed a moment to blame someone that wasn't herself.

As she looked into eyes of the sea and deep mahogany framed with drenched hair, eyes that were filled with such complex despair, she realized that perhaps she wasn't the only one hurting. That maybe, they were just as upset about her circumstances as she was. She understood now why River had wanted her to come back with them: not to fix what had happened, but to give her a chance to make things right if she wished. The thought had her lurching forward, two strong sets of arms wasting no time in curling around and clutching onto her. They didn't say a word, simply held her as she did the same for them. They smelled like rain, rain and smoke and the earth.

She took that time to let her mind wander, leading her to reflect on her inner self of the previous days. When had she become so mopey and overrun by her emotions? What happened to the girl who survived The Voice's torment with confidence and who had unlimited determination? The girl who was resilient and had the ability to tackle any obstacle thrown at her? What happened to the girl who grit her teeth and pushed through, even if it hurt, even when it felt like there was no hope? When had that girl disappeared? Kaitlyn wanted her back.

Maybe, this, right here, was the first step to finding her again.

Perhaps all she needed was a little nudge in the right direction. A little prod to get her to open her eyes. The return of the two boys an instigator for this very epiphany. But she wouldn't take anything else from them. She would find herself on her own. She didn't need anyone else to save her. She already knew how to save herself perfectly fine. She'd done it before, so what was one more time?

CHAPTER FIFTEEN
NOT A GOODBYE

"Is that everything, Wes?!" River hollered from the back of the car where he stood arranging all their belongings in the trunk.

"Yep, just this bag here and we're all set!" Wes chirped with a cheerfulness that River could tell was a little forced.

Wes rounded the car and plopped the remaining bag in with the rest of the stuff. River slammed the trunk with a resounding 'thunk!' that held such an air of finality to it, that he felt his throat tighten. He glanced to the side, where Kaitlyn stood leaning against a nearby tree. She had this far off look in her eyes, unfocused, like there was something only she was capable of seeing. The resemblance to Wes was almost uncanny. Yet, there was a funny little smile adorning her lips, and it brought him back to this morning.

Kaitlyn had deviated from her usual morning routine. Instead of sitting by the firepit and patiently waiting for them to rise, she'd pranced circles around their tent, beating the polyester walls with sticks while making animalistic grunts, and chanting in some garbled language like she was performing some freaky ritualistic sacrifice.

It was safe to say that when River woke with a start, he had promptly wondered if he was about to die.

Not a second later, with River still disoriented, Wes had shot up into a sitting position with his hands held up in front of him like he was about to karate chop something, turning his head back and forth, rasping, "Waz dat?" If

River hadn't just woken up, he would have blatantly laughed at his friend, hair sticking up at comical angles and whose eyes were squinted so narrow he probably couldn't even see. In that moment, River didn't think Wes could've hit the broad side of a barn, much less fend off any crazed cannibal attackers.

When the creepy nonsense from outside ceased and a voice hollered, "Rise and shine, ladies!" River relaxed immediately, recognizing Kaitlyn's raspy voice.

Wes too, had seemed relieved, if the way he'd collapsed back onto his sleeping bag was anything to go by.

"You weirdo, do you even sleep?" Wes had called out.

The only response was a snort followed by a stick rebounding off the side of the tent.

It was then, albeit with far too long of a delay, River registered that he'd just been called a lady...by a lady. Ugh, it was too early for this.

He had crawled out of his sleeping bag and unzipped the tent. He groaned, his suspicions being correct. The sky was a dark periwinkle, the sun just barely having peaked its infuriating little head over the horizon. Honestly, it couldn't have been any later than 5 A.M.

River had found himself glaring half-heartedly at the girl standing a few feet away, a deceivingly innocent look on her face. His eyes sharpened on the stick dangling unassumingly from her hands that were clasped behind her back. She was rocking back and forth on her bare feet, looking all too pleased with herself.

He had given her a deadpan, "You're a little monster, you know that?"

She'd blinked her big bluish-green eyes at him, wide and disarming. "I've no idea what you mean."

Then she'd sashayed off, weaving the stick mockingly through the air behind her. River had wanted to laugh–he almost did–but it was still too early and he was trying not to think about the fact that in less than 8 hours, he and

Wes would be leaving.

"You're brooding again."

River jumped, whirling around to face the voice while retorting what had recently become his steadfast response, "Am not!"

As the pair started to verbally spar back and forth, Kaitlyn couldn't help but silently snicker at River's choice of outfit. He was wearing cornflower blue skinny jeans with a bright white shirt and cherry red high-top converse. He was all flaming red, overly saturated blues and blinding whites. With all three paired together on the same person, the full image was absolutely ridiculous. Kaitlyn had a hard time keeping a straight face as she watched the ginger gesticulate wildly with his hands, the single stud earring on his ear flashing in the mid-morning light.

"He looks like a Rocket Pop," she mused in her head.

At least, she thought she did.

The two boys abruptly looked at her, and for a split second she was entirely convinced they'd read her mind. The notion was quickly corrected, however, when Wes slowly gave River a full, thorough once over before a leering grin split his face.

River's mouth fell open, offended, when he registered the comment was directed at him. He then proceeded to give himself the once-over, scrutinizing his own appearance.

Kaitlyn probably looked akin to a deer caught in the headlights as she stared at the boys with wide eyes, lips smashed together. No mind readers here apparently, just a girl whose mouth refused to ask permission before speaking.

Eventually, River eyed his two friends, who were currently wearing twin insufferable smirks, with an unimpressed look.

Wes held up a quaking hand for Kaitlyn to high five. She only paused for a split second before indulging him.

River just shook his head, disbelieving, "You both suck

ass. I need to stop spending so much time with you."

"You couldn't stay away even if you tried, Rivera," Wes cooed, knowing he'd pay for it later.

Mildly appalled, River's eyes widened at the same time Kaitlyn raised an eyebrow and repeated doubtfully, "Rivera?" as she shifted her weight to one foot.

River closed his eyes, pained. "It's my name," he grumbled, looking off to the side.

Kaitlyn's expression remained unchanged. "That's an actual name?"

"Yes, clearly" the male burst exasperatedly.

Kaitlyn held up her hands in surrender, though an amused smirk adorned her face. "Touchy," she drawled.

The behavior reminded River so much of Dylan that for a moment, he was certain she was the one who was standing in front of him.

The illusion was broken, however, when Kaitlyn started bouncing circles around him while chanting childishly, 'Ri-vera, Ri-vera, Ri-vera.'

Wes slowly crossed his arms with precise exaggeration, his eyebrows shooting into his hairline as Kaitlyn started to poke at his friend.

River batted her away when a jab landed particularly hard in his stomach, trying and failing to stifle his laughter.

Snickering, Kaitlyn relented. After the three of them took a few moments to settle down, River and Wes began to make their way to the car.

River attempted to open the passenger side door, but found it locked. "Dude," he called to Wes, who was patting down his jean pockets with a puzzled expression.

A faint jingle had both males turning their heads. They were met with the sight of Kaitlyn tauntingly dangling a set of car keys from one finger.

"Looking for these?"

Wes furrowed his brows in slight disbelief, "How did

you—"

River wolf-whistled, "I'm almost impressed."

The three stared each other down, frozen in an intense staring contest, brown and blue clashing with turquoise. All that was missing was an old western backdrop and a lone tumbleweed.

Kaitlyn took off like the devil himself was on her heels.

River and Wes bolted in pursuit a second later, chasing Kaitlyn around the vacant parking lot.

"Give us the damn keys!"

"Hah! You gotta catch me first!"

Not much later, both boys were bent over, hands braced on their knees and panting loudly. Kaitlyn made sure to take her sweet time as she moseyed up to them and pristinely sat down on the parking lot near their forms.

As in sync as it was uncanny, they both shifted their heads to look at her and said, breathless, "This is your fault."

She snorted, stretching out her tanned legs across the pavement and tossing them the keys, which Wes snatched from the air.

The boys eventually came to join her in a similar position, River on her left and Wes on her right. Filled with content, all three of them gazed up at the puffy white clouds drifting across the blue sky, neither one of them wanting the moment to end.

"You're still a Rocket Pop," Kaitlyn drawled with a smirk.

"I'm never going to let you live this down," Wes piped up with a teasing grin.

River rolled his eyes, but he was smiling. "There are worse things to be called, I suppose."

~~~~~~~~~

"You can still come with us you know," Wes offered softly.

Kaitlyn smiled at him sadly and shook her head.

Wes nodded in solemn understanding, the low purr of
~~~~~~~~~

the car engine providing bittersweet background noise.

She gazed into his brown eyes, an ache steadily growing in her chest, tightening until it became nearly impossible to breathe. But something in those mahogany depths lined with shimmering bronze reminded Kaitlyn of home, the one that she no longer knew, and the pain loosened its hold on her windpipe a little.

River hopped out of the car then, coming around to join them at the back. He'd switched his blue jeans out for charcoal gray, and Kaitlyn couldn't resist giving his pants a pointed look.

The ginger flushed high on his cheeks, the pinkness coloring up to his ears. "Shut up," he groused.

Kaitlyn flicked the stud on his left ear lobe with a teasing quirk of the lips and River couldn't help but laugh. She looked uncharacteristically fond of the red-haired male, and he found himself getting choked up.

The only thing he could think as he looked at her, was that she was one hell of a miracle. With her tousled auburn hair framing her face; her drapey animal skin dress; her tan, freckled skin; the sharp angles of her face; and her enchanting sea green eyes that flashed with a wildness unlike anything he'd ever seen. It stole his breath away, just how wild and free she really was. This girl, who ran with wolves through the trees, who had survived what should have been impossible. Life had smacked her in the face, knocked her to rock bottom and gave little opportunity or support to ever climb out. She'd been tormented by a malevolent entity that had wanted to consume her. She'd been traumatized by it, both The Voice and the sheer solitude she had to endure all these years. He couldn't even begin to comprehend what that must have been like, could probably live a hundred lifetimes and still never understand her pain, all that agony and emotional torture. Any other person wouldn't have made it, which is what made her so remarkable.

Kaitlyn, wild and beautiful Kaitlyn, was still standing,

standing right in front of him. Maybe she was a little bent out of shape, rough around the edges and cracked in places that may never fully heal, but not broken.

Never broken.

River suddenly understood why Wes didn't want her to be real.

Unable to resist the urge any longer, River dragged Kaitlyn into a hug and squeezed her so hard he was sure he heard her ribs creak. She didn't complain though, reciprocating as good as she got. It wasn't long before Wes was hauled into the embrace as well.

"We'll come back and visit, promise," River mumbled into Kaitlyn's hair.

Wes firmly nodded his agreement.

Kaitlyn smiled, letting herself bask in the warmth of the hold for a moment longer before gently detangling herself from them.

A look was shared between the three of them, and there was an unspoken understanding that River and Wes wouldn't go blabbing about Kaitlyn to anyone. It was their secret, just between them...at least for now.

"Don't worry about me," she said in a slightly tremulous voice, vision blurry. She gave a wobbly smile. "Go live your lives. And besides..." She threw a look over her shoulder, her eyes landing on the dark silhouette of Midnight sitting patiently at the treeline, waiting.

She turned back to the boys, gave them each a nudge. "You won't be leaving me here alone."

Kaitlyn ushered two very unwilling males into their car, insistent that they get going so they made it back home on time. When they were both situated in the car, Wes in the driver's seat with River on the passenger side, the redhead rolled down his window. Just as Kaitlyn was pulling away, he seized her wrist and tugged her back closer to the car. He waited until she met his eyes before stating firmly, "This isn't goodbye, got it?" He gave her arm a little shake. "We'll be back, hopefully sooner than you think."

Kaitlyn nodded mutely, afraid that if she opened her mouth, some pitiful sob would claw its way out.

"Say it," Wes demanded.

"Say what?" Kaitlyn croaked.

His dark eyes met hers over River. "Not a goodbye. Say it."

She held his intense gaze, willing herself to not look away.

Forcing strength into her voice, she repeated quietly but unyielding, "Not a goodbye."

Wes nodded his approval as River stroked his thumb lightly over the inside of her wrist before dropping it all together. They both flashed her blinding smiles as she backed away to give them room to pull out, and she couldn't help but return it, even if hers was less confident.

She waved them off, eyes trailing the car as it exited the parking lot and disappeared around a bend.

Her arm fell heavily at her side, the smile vanishing from her face in an instant as she stared longingly at the place the car had once been.

She wouldn't cry. She wouldn't. This wasn't a goodbye. It was a beginning. The beginning of something new, something to look forward to. It was incredible how close the three of them had become in less than a week. It made her want to laugh when she compared how she felt about them when they first arrived to how she felt now. The shift was almost comical, but she couldn't find it in herself to care. The connection they'd formed was genuine, no matter how brief a time it had been established in.

They'd swept into her life like a whirlwind and upturned nearly everything she'd known. Although it had ticked her off, she was glad they'd come here and made her see herself a little differently, forcing her to open her eyes. The only thing she could think was that she was thankful they went camping with their families all those years ago, because it all led them here, led them to her.

She wasn't going to give them all of the credit for helping her start her real healing process, because only she could heal herself. She was the only one who could pick up the pieces and place them back together in a picture that held a semblance of herself. She realized that she was not broken, severely cracked, yes, but not broken. The boys' appearance had not been the killing blow, but merely a catalyst, making her believe again that the earthquakes that had initially shaken her foundation, that had knocked her off her feet, weren't going to destroy her. Knowing them made her stronger.

So no, she was not broken. It would take time for her to feel whole again, to truly start to fill the chasm inside her rather than cover it up, but that was one thing she did have: time. It stretched out before her, vast and infinite, full of so much promise. She wouldn't pretend that she didn't already miss them, that the loss of their joyous presence left a bittersweet pang in her bones, but she would see them again, and that was enough. Finally, something was enough.

She felt free, hopeful as the future stretched out before her. She took one more glance at the place where River and Wes's car had disappeared; one day that car would appear again, would pull into the parking lot into the exact spot it had previously occupied. Potentially sooner rather than later, in fact.

"One day," the voice in her head whispered silkenly, filled with silent elation.

Kaitlyn smiled, warm and bright, "Yes, one day."

Then she turned around and made her way over to Midnight. The wolf gazed up at her with such keen awareness in her eyes that they almost resembled a human.

Kaitlyn smiled fondly, closed mouthed and sweet. She stretched out her hand and Midnight met her halfway, pressing her wet nose to the girl's open palm.

"Let's go home, Midnight," Kaitlyn said.

The black wolf woofed softly, as if in agreement, and together, the two of them spirited off through the forest.

The echo in their wake was Kaitlyn's joyful laughter. It twirled through the air and up over the trees, soared on the wind currents to places where no one was around to hear it.

It was a sound that was wild and free.

Kaitlyn Amor was strong and resilient. She would continue to persevere, to get back up if she was knocked down. She did not need anyone else to hold her up, to fix her, because she was perfect just the way she was. If she had a problem, she would fix it herself, even if she had outside encouragement, in the end, it was ultimately her responsibility to save herself, and she would continue to do so. She was the guardian of this forest. Would protect it until she drew her last breath and returned to the earth from which had become her true home.

This was how legends were born.

The legend of the wild child.

EPILOGUE

The first part of the drive was silent, save for the occasional soft sniffle from River's side of the car. Wes had wordlessly handed him a tissue that he had seemingly pulled out of thin air, to which River batted away, keeping his face hidden.

Wes blinked with significant purpose, attempting to clear the wetness from his own eyes so that he wouldn't inadvertently crash the car.

Why was this so difficult? Hell, they'd only known the girl for less than a week! Though that didn't make it any less real, and perhaps that was why it hurt so much, because no longer was she just an idea in their heads, something they believed to just be a dream, a figment of their childhood overactive imaginations. No, she was a reality, solid through and through. A walking miracle.

"We're pathetic," Wes said around a forced chuckle.

River turned to look at him. Out of the corner of his eyes, Wes could see his eyes were bright and nose slightly red, but his face was dry.

"No," he croaked, clearing his throat before trying again. "No."

Silence.

"Okay maybe a little."

Wes gave a laugh, shaking his head.

The strange atmosphere broke when one of the boys' phones buzzed. Sluggishly, River moved to dig his device out of his duffle bag pocket from the back. He caught Wes's eyes as he resituated himself in his seat. They shared a small smile. They'd see her again, and that was all that mattered. This wasn't the end.

The rest of the drive home was quiet and uneventful, and when they pulled up to Wes's house, their entire entourage of friends burst forth from the front door and rushed out to greet them. It was an unexpected, and frankly unneeded, welcome home party, but neither of them could complain. The boisterous energy of the other teenagers was contagious and had River and Wes's sadness all but vanishing. Until Dylan nudged them both suggestively and brought up the wild girl.

Wes would have anyone know that he was an excellent liar. River, on the other hand...he side-eyed the male in question, who was sporting the most forced poker face Wes had ever seen.

'Jeez, he looks constipated,' Wes thought to himself.

He suppressed a sigh, *'Can't be helped I suppose.'*

Wes went on to tell them all that there was no girl in that forest, and it was probably just a dream that they all coincidentally had. Everyone ignored Amy's smug "hmph."

When they finished catching up, everyone headed inside, Dylan complaining about having to put up with Josh *and only Josh* for a *whole week.*

Josh, in all his blond-haired glory, hung back and shot River and Wes a suspicious look, scrutinizing them from head to toe. Wes kept very still, and River willed his face to remain blank as his palms became clammy and a drip of sweat ran down the back of his neck. But Josh said nothing, and the suspicion in his ridiculously blue eyes transitioned into something akin to knowing, like he was all too aware of the fact that his two friends had been lying straight through their teeth. The blond teen mimed a finger to his lips and turned to follow everyone else inside.

River and Wes shared dumbfounded looks. Although Josh sometimes came off as a little slow and inherently idiotic by nature, the guy had his moments of insight. The boys weren't worried though. If nothing else, while it may not seem like it, Josh was a loyal friend. If someone entrusted him with a secret that no one else was to know, he would take that secret to his grave unless permitted to do otherwise. Sure, they hadn't told him, hadn't even hinted at the fact that the wild girl from their dreams was actually real, but somehow, he knew. And Wes and River would neither confirm nor deny his suspicions. Maybe one day the two of them would tell the others about Kaitlyn, but today was not that day.

River looped an arm around Wes's neck, laughing as he started to exaggeratedly step toward the house, pulling Wes along with him.

Before they could pass through the doorway though, River halted them and glanced up at his taller friend.

Quietly, voice soft with hope, he whispered, "When?"

Wes smiled, bright and purposeful, as he rustled River's hair and asked, "Beginning of next month?"

River nodded. "It's settled then."

They both stepped inside, the door closing behind them with a soft click.

This wasn't an ending.

Rather, it was only the beginning.

No one knew how it came to be, nor from whose web the wild tale had been spun, but it was there, growing until there was not a single soul in existence that did not know it.

The Wild Child.

A young female guardian who roamed the deep, uncharted forest of Oregon, a pack of wolves regularly following at her back. She detained the unseen evils that once preyed upon the families who entered the wilderness. No longer could their existence prevail so long as she was around. Her very presence made them tremble. Her grit sent them running.

The story wove its way through hearts and souls. Some, often adults, surmised that it was merely a story, a myth conjured up by the mind of a creative force. Others, often children, or those tousling with adolescence, persisted that she was real, a few even claiming they'd seen her with their own eyes.

She became a thing of bedtime stories, a means of comfort and idolization for young children. "There's nothing to be afraid of, The Wild Child is out there somewhere, and she will protect you, always."

The rumor often led others to seek out proof of her being. Teenagers would traverse into the woodland attached to their backyards, camping gear on their backs and over their shoulders. They'd stay out for nights on end, only to never see a thing out of place. But some say that as you are leaving your camping spot, if you look over your shoulder at the right moment, you will see her standing there in a dress delicately crafted from the skin of a doe, watching you leave with entrancing blue-green eyes. The second you blink, she will be gone, not a single trace of her left behind.

Skeptics surmised it as the mind playing tricks, making people see what they wanted to see. Others would adamantly insist that what they had seen was real.

Be as it may, it appeared unlikely that a concrete answer would ever be established.

Of course, many different versions of the story began to arise as the tale of The Wild Child was stretched and warped to fit others' ideals. They would play up the story or add in embellished details to make the ordeal more grand. Some would even invent an origin of how she came to be in the forest in the first place.

Eventually, it became so distorted that listeners were unsure what was the original tale and what were the frivolous additions used to decorate it. Despite all these versions, the question still remained: just who was this wild girl, and where did she actually come from?

There were only two souls who knew the answer.

The only ones who knew the truth.

Not only did they know the truth, but also personally knew the star of the legend herself. It was for that very reason that they never attempted to divert the rumor in any way.

Because once upon a time, a girl named Kaitlyn told them that to the outside world, she didn't exist, that she was forgotten. But now, under the ambiguous cover of legend, she did.

Even though she was without a specific name, the world once again knew who she was. Never again would she be forgotten or erased from the minds of society, and it was all from the result of selflessly saving others from her own fate despite the ache that always plagued her chest upon watching them go.

Always remember, that legends never die.

Remember Kaitlyn Amor.

Remember The Wild Child.

BONUS CHAPTER
THE VOICE

Where I come from, there is only Darkness. Many of my kin have deemed It worthy of the title: The Nothing. I call it by no name. To me, The Darkness as a physical entity simply *is*.

There was Darkness before my birth, and there is Darkness after my end. Those in The Darkness have been reverted to a state of non-existence. All of us who were thwarted, all of the consumed souls within our entities end up here. We become integrated with The Dark. This Dark that The Creator fashioned from Its own being. The Creator has been absent for millennia, and none of Its children can fathom what may have become of It.

I hold no concern. If The Creator has gone away, then there is a valid reason for it.

The state of non-existence is not permanent, but its duration varies from entity to entity. It is not certain what one must do to overcome this state, only that one must display a great amount of will and manifest strength from depleted reserves.

There is no rhyme nor reason, as I believe the human saying goes.

Time does not pass here; The Dark is suspended in a moment long before the earth's creation. Its age reaches beyond that of the galaxy, perhaps even that of the universe. The Creator once revealed to me a vast time ago that Its birth shared the birth of the very first atom of matter.

I suspect my own relief from this non-existence is so far within the after, that it is out of my sight entirely.

"You have lost your spirit," a relatively young entity, a mere child, informed me some time after I'd returned to non-existence.

'That blasted human pest,' I recalled.

"I can feel the span of the child's will, the ferocity of her protectiveness. It pushes even as I no longer am. I think I am done now," I replied, distancing from the juvenile entity.

I am the eldest, the first of many The Creator fashioned. My existence within the earthly plane persisted from my birth. My life, as humans would call it, has been long. I am tired, and while it would be possible for me to tap into other versions of the earthly plane, I am faced with disinterest.

I do not wish to meddle with earth's affairs any longer, and in this state of non-existence, I am no longer plagued by hunger. Here, I require no sustenance.

That child wielded more strength than I had anticipated. Perhaps it would have been more beneficial to my existence if I had merely let that one move on. It had been abnormally troublesome to dispose of the family and their memories as well.

Now I will rest. I will subject myself to the archaic state of non-thought. A state of non-anything. I will once again become inanimate matter. Consider it a permanent hibernation, if you will. Only The Creator possesses the power to breathe existence back into me from the state of non-thought. I suspect The Creator has withdrawn into Its own eternity, and is unlikely to ever return.

I prefer this way of things.

One might harbor the notion that I have lost, and that the child has won. This is false. The Darkness is a being; It has existed long before the birth of time and It will exist long after time ceases. It will persist when the earth is no more, when the galaxy will one day collide with The Andromeda, and when the universe will progress into a state of such disorder, that it will destroy itself. The Darkness will be here until The Creator resolves to eradicate It.

In my sole stead, many will take my place. Our numbers are far greater than the existence of all celestial bodies. Our entities are so vast, that there is not a single living thing, nor object, large enough to contain them.

The Darkness is the before, the now, and the after.

Not even Light itself may conquer It.

ACKNOWLEDGEMENTS

As something that originally started as a short story to fulfill my own creative outlet, I never thought that it would see the light of day, much less be published. The process it took to get here has been a journey of tenacity, to say the least. After many abandoned thought processes and rewrites over the years, only to realize my writing style had changed, in some ways drastically, there were many lulls in the production. One thing that always stayed the same, however, was my underlying love for otherworldly concepts in my writing and for bringing my characters to life. They are a part of me, an extension of my imagination, and I get to know them as much as the readers. To me, writing is like getting to know a new person you feel you've known for a lifetime and then missing them when they must go at the turn of the final page.

I'd like to thank the following people who have helped make this little musing of mine into a reality:

My publisher, New Book Authors Publishing, Em Hughes, who provided such helpful feedback and insight into the art of writing. Thank you for seeing something within these pages, for seeing what this story could be. I owe the finished product to you.

My editor, Alyssa W., who gave important tips, comments, and edits regarding how to better my writing. Any remaining errors are entirely my own, cause sometimes I just suck at grammar and use too many words.

Michael Farina and Devon Duffy for taking the time to read through one of my early drafts and providing invaluable feedback and suggestions. I will always have an unending gratitude to you both for teaching me beyond the scope of a typical English classroom.

And lastly, a big shout out to my mom, Melissa, for tirelessly reading and rereading my drafts and for inspiring me to take the action to turn this dream into a reality. This book never would have made it past the idea stage if not for her unyielding encouragement and support.

ABOUT THE AUTHOR

Olivia Krimin, or Via, as her friends call her, is from the small town Indiana, Pennsylvania. She is currently a pre-med undergraduate student at the University of Rochester pursuing a Bachelor's degree in Neuroscience with a double minor in Ethical Philosophy and Chemistry and a concentration in Psychopathology. Outside of academics, she loves reading, coffee shops, collecting poetry books, traveling and exploring new places in nature, and has been involved in various genres of dance for fourteen years. She can routinely be found awake well into the early hours of the morning or studying while tucked into a cozy corner of one of the campus libraries. Wild Child is her first novel.